A love that burns bright…

"How do you do that to me?" I whispered against his mouth. "How do you burn me up and rebuild me every single time?"

"You're my phoenix," he said, his lips smoldering my skin. "And I'm yours."

The Brothers Wilde Serials

The Untamed Series:

Untamed

Out of Control

Escaped Artist

Wild at Heart

Rebel Roused

Novels by Victoria Green

Silver Heart

Novels by Jen Meyers

Anywhere

The Intangible Series

Intangible

Imaginable

Indomitable (an *Intangible* novella)

untamed

episode 5: rebel roused

victoria green & jen meyers

rebel
roused

one
Dare

High.

I was high as a fucking kite, drunk on life, and feeling truly alive for the first time in months. My world was filled with color—every hue and shade imaginable—brushing over the darkness, brightening the grays and blacks that had shrouded my life.

My father was out. So was Ree's.

We'd fucking won.

I'd given my statement to the police, my fingers drumming on my leg the whole time, my body itching to hop back on my bike and cross the river back to Ree. Even as I told them what I knew about my dad, I was picturing Ree packing up her stuff, imagining how she would fill the void in my apartment. In my heart. In my life.

We'd fucking WON.

I crowed as I swerved through traffic, speeding

over the 59th Street bridge into Queens, the engine roaring beneath me. Ree and I were free to start a life together. Our own life, where happiness had no boundaries and rain was followed by a fucking rainbow—not shitstorm after shitstorm.

It had been years since I'd felt this grounded. I was ready for this life with Ree. Ready for commitment. Ready to make her mine forever.

I patted the front of my black leather jacket, feeling the little square lump in the inside pocket—a little extra stop I'd made after the precinct. The small velvet box held the first step toward our future, and I was going to give it to her tonight. No waiting for the perfect moment. No planning some staged grand gesture. No hesitating.

She was mine and I was hers. Nearly losing her to that bomb had changed everything.

Had it only been days since then? It felt like a whole fucking lifetime had passed. An avalanche of game-changing things had occurred: so many struggles coming to an end, problems being solved, loose ends getting tied up.

We were done. Finally and forever done. With blackmail. With games. With everybody and their fucking uncles getting in our way.

The bomb had been rock bottom. Now, there was nowhere to go but up.

In fact, we were already on our way—we had the mayor's vow that my father was going back to prison. The police had assured me my testimony would help keep him there. Two counts of murder. The bastard would rot like he should have the first time around.

No more sick, twisted surprises.

Real, uncomplicated happiness was finally ours.

The sun shone warm against my skin, brightening what was already a perfect fall day. Perhaps after we got Ree's stuff settled into my place, we'd head out to the south shore, spend the weekend out on Long Island. The two of us, away from everything and everyone. No distractions. And definitely no clothes.

The thought had me grinning.

I parked my bike outside of Rex's house, then walked around to the outside entrance that led up to Ree's apartment. Taking the steps two at a time, her name was on my lips before I even opened the front door. I was desperate to see her, touch her, hear her voice, fill myself up with her presence.

But she was nowhere to be found. Her bags were mostly packed, the bed was stripped, but the place was empty. Knowing my girl and her love for art, she was probably in Rex's studio, quietly watching him paint with a cup of tea in hand, waiting for me.

Aside from his models and me, Ree was the only person Rex had ever allowed in the room while he painted, and I was pretty damn sure he preferred her presence to mine. They could spend hours lost in their own world, debating artists, styles, and paintings.

With everything that had happened the past few months, I was more than grateful that Rex had been Ree's knight in paint-speckled armor. He'd been my savior and hers. And while I loved my family with every fiber of my being, Ree and Rex were the two most important people in my life. The fact that they had formed such a close bond meant a lot to me.

The door down to Rex's studio was wide open, which was more than a little odd for the old recluse, and as soon as I started down the stairs I could feel it.

Something was wrong.

Terribly fucking wrong.

Sheets and towels lay strewn all over the bottom of the stairs and Rex's studio was trashed. His lights were smashed, easel tipped over and broken, and a crushed cell phone lay on the floor. A bright red trail of paint led into the house.

Oh, Jesus. Not paint.

Blood.

Fear shot through me as I chased the crimson path, ripping through the house, terrified I was about to come face-to-face with my worst nightmare. Heart pounding, panic had me by the balls and was squeezing the fucking life out of me. This had to be just a bad dream and I would wake up any minute now.

It had to be.

Because...this couldn't be happening. Not now. Not when everything was finally working out in our favor. If that was Ree's—

"*Dare...*" Rex coughed out my name, his voice weak, and for a brief instant I was frozen in anguish.

He was lying on the living room floor, his head and shoulders propped up crookedly against the bottom of the couch. A cordless phone in one hand, he clutched his abdomen with the other. His bone-white face was a chilling contrast to his blood-soaked shirt.

No, no...FUCK NO.

In an instant, I was across the room, kneeling next to him, and pressing my hand over his to keep the pressure on his wound.

"Dare…" His voice was whisper thin, pain vibrating through it, hitting me hard, shattering my heart.

"Don't talk." I pulled out my cell phone. "I'm calling an ambulance right now. It's going to be okay. You're going to be fine, Rex. You're going to be okay, you hear me?"

He *had* to be. He couldn't die. Save for Ree, no one in my life had ever believed in me as much as Rex. He was the reason I had a life that was worth living. He was my father in every sense of the word. And he had to be okay, goddammit.

Rex lifted the phone in his hand. "Already…called." I could hear the dispatch repeat that help was coming as Rex's eyes closed, then fluttered open. "He…has…Ree."

I didn't ask who he was talking about.

My father's revenge.

The phone dropped out of his hand and his head lolled to the side.

"Rex, no! Stay with me. *Please!*" My vision blurred as I shifted him into my arms and reached for his hand. His grip was too weak—no, *please god, no*—and his eyes weren't focusing on anything. "You hear me, Rex? Don't you fucking die on me!"

There wasn't enough air in this room, my chest heaved, pain crushing me as I held him.

"What's going on?" He shook his head slightly, confusion crossing his face. "Where am I? Who's here?"

"It's me, Rex, and you're home. You've been hurt." I squeezed his hand. "Help is coming. You have to hold on just a little longer. Okay? Just a little longer. Please!"

My face was drenched with tears, my hands and clothes soaked in blood. Too much blood, and it wasn't stopping. Our palms pressed against his stomach, but it kept flowing. Why wouldn't it stop?

Just a few minutes more, I kept telling myself. Just until the paramedics got here. They could save him if he'd just hang on for a little longer.

I leaned in close to him. "Please, Rex. Please just…don't die."

His deep green gaze found my face and recognition bloomed within his eyes. "Dare…" A slight smile lifted the corners of his mouth. "I love you, my son. Always have." A tear slid down his cheek.

"Shit, Rex. You know I love you." I held him tighter as my throat started to close. "Just hang on, old man. *Please. For me.*"

He started to nod, but then the light in his eyes dimmed. Fuck…it was going out.

"No…Rex…"

His smile slipped, all expression erased from his face as his body went limp. A small stream of blood trickled down his chin.

"NO. *REX!*" I shook my head over and over again. "Don't go! Please! *NO!*"

There was a banging on the front door, but I couldn't respond. Sobs wracked my body as I held his lifeless form in my arms

My teacher, my friend, my true father.

Gone.

It wasn't supposed to be like this. It was over. It was fucking OVER. We'd taken care of everything. My dad couldn't blow all our hard work to pieces now that we'd won. This wasn't the way it was supposed to go.

By the time the paramedics pried me away from Rex, I wasn't in control of my body or mind. Hurt and rage flowed through my veins, engulfing me, scorching my heart, filling me with deadly determination.

I watched as they checked for a pulse, looked for any signs of life, unable to answer their questions as my mind churned, my eyes never straying from Rex's still form.

This would be the last thing my father ever did. His legacy ended now.

I would hunt him down, and make him pay for what he did to Rex.

And if he hurt Ree in the meantime?

All the gods in the world wouldn't be able to save him from my wrath.

two
Reagan

My head ached.

That was the first thing I noticed.

The second was that I didn't even care.

A very familiar floaty feeling enveloped me. I could feel every molecule of air going into my lungs as I listened to the music of cars going by on my right. Though I could sense every inch of my body, it didn't feel like my limbs really belonged to me. And I tried my damnedest to figure out why that felt *wrong*. Once upon a time, I remembered it feeling so, so *right*.

Slowly, I opened my eyes. Darkness sped by, punctuated by lights too bright for my eyes. I brought my hands up to shield my face.

"Give her another hit." The voice was hard and rough. Male. And I tried to place where I'd heard it before. A fuzzy memory prodded the back of my mind. Something had happened…but I couldn't remember what. My brain refused to focus on anything for very long.

And why the hell was I even bothering to fight the haze? There was a reason, I was sure of it. An important reason. Fuck. What was it?

Before I could chase away the smoke obscuring my thoughts, something pricked my arm. The sting was followed by a delicious feeling of serenity, and I closed my eyes again, surrendering to the clouds in my mind.

Voices argued from far away, echoing in my mind as I tried to surface. It was like I was swimming through quicksand—the harder I tried to come up to consciousness, the more I was dragged down.

But little by little, I made progress. The angry voices became clearer as light filtered into my awareness. Shit. The noise hurt like hell. I immediately wanted to shrink away from it all, yell at the loud voices to go away, but it was so freaking hard to get my mouth to move, I couldn't tell whether I had made even a sound. I could barely breathe. My chest felt like it was being crushed and the air felt too thick.

Then a hand grabbed my jaw, and my eyes flew

open. My heart slammed against my ribcage as the man in front of me shoved a pill into my mouth, and then held it closed.

"Swallow," he said, his voice as gruff as sandpaper.

I squinted into the morning light barely streaming through the dirty windows, and tried to figure out why someone was giving me pills. Had I been hurt? Was I in the hospital?

"Swallow, bitch. NOW." He clamped my nose shut so I couldn't breathe.

I clawed at his hands and tried to kick out my feet, but someone grabbed them. Christ. What the fuck was going on? The light was killing my head, and my brain was all fogged up. I struggled, my lungs burning, darkness crowding the edges of my vision.

"Open her mouth," another voice said. "If we give her a drink, she'll swallow." Chills ran down my spine. I *knew* that voice.

They laughed, and someone grabbed my arms and held them down, while the first guy pried my jaw open. I didn't have time to breathe before water was poured down my throat, and I was sputtering and coughing.

And swallowing.

They let go roughly, and I thought for sure I

was going to cough up a lung. When I finally caught my breath, I was staring into the dead-cold eyes of Dare's father.

The floodgates opened and everything came rushing back.

Daren shooting Rex and then…the blood. Oh, god, all the blood that was spreading so fast even before they dragged me out of his studio and threw me into their car. That image was burned into my brain: Rex lying there helpless, surprise and confusion on his face as he clutched at his stomach, his head shaking in disbelief. Tears stung my eyes. I only hoped someone heard the shot and got there in time.

Because Rex had to survive. He HAD to.

I glanced around the room—where the fuck had they taken me? It looked like an old warehouse. Rusty metal walls thirty feet high were lined with filthy, small-paned windows all along the roofline. Junk was littered throughout, as if the place had been abandoned a long time ago.

And it was quiet. Disturbingly so. No sounds of cars nor people. Fuck. Not a chance of someone hearing me if I screamed. Still, I had to try.

Drawing in a raspy breath, I opened my mouth, but no sound came out. My throat was as dry as the fucking desert, and my body and mind felt like

I had no control over them. As my vision started to swim, my limbs began to feel weightless. I was floating.

Higher, higher, *higher*...

God, what had they given me? I was never going to get out of here if they kept me drugged. And I had to get out of here. I had to keep Dare far, far away from the madman in front of me.

"Wh...where...?" I tried to speak the full sentence, but the words were getting stuck somewhere between my brain and lips.

Daren stepped forward, bringing his face close to mine. "Don't you worry about a thing, Princess," he said. "You just tell me everything I want to know, and you'll die quickly." He laughed. "Let's start with Dare's phone number. He needs to see this with his own eyes."

"Fuck..." My words slurred. "...off."

There was a sharp sting around my eye and my head ricocheted backwards, banging against the cement floor.

Then everything went blessedly black.

When I surfaced again, it was dark. I glanced up at the windows, where the sky was just beginning to lighten. The warehouse was deathly quiet. A light burned bright where two men sat staring at their phones in silence on the other side of the building, but I was cloaked in shadow.

God, was this it? Was this my chance?

Keeping my gaze on them, I slowly—*painstakingly*—got to my feet. My right eye felt weird, and I reached up to touch my face. Jesus. The whole side was puffed up and tender, throbbing under my touch. I couldn't even see the hand in front of that side of my face. My eye was swollen shut, my cheek sticky with blood.

I glanced around, looking for the nearest door. Shit, it was all the way across the room. Not near the two guys, thank god, yet not close enough for me to slip out with ease.

Sticking to the shadows, I took a couple of steps toward the door and paused. The two were deep in some angry conversation now, oblivious to me. My heart hammered louder the closer I got to the door. It was dark out and I had no idea where I was, even what state I was in, but if I got through that door, I would run like the fucking devil was chasing me.

Because, most likely, he would be.

My life depended on the next few seconds.

Here goes—

"Do you really think we're going to let you just walk out the door? You gotta be fucking kidding me."

My heart lodged in my throat, and I turned to see Daren behind me, leaning casually against a shadowy corner of the wall.

Fuck. Me.

He slinked out of the darkness, sneering. "You think it's going to be *that* easy to get away from me, Princess?" He threw back his head and laughed. "My son obviously told you nothing about me."

"He told me plenty."

His eyebrows shot up and his eyes brightened with interest. "Do tell."

I kept my mouth shut and glared at him, realizing too late I'd just given him another reason to kill me. Like he needed any more.

"No? Well then, I'll have to leave it up to my imagination." He tapped a finger to his temple. "And I've got a wild one. In fact, I've been dreaming up all sorts of fun things to do to you while that shit-for-brains bastard son of mine watches." Stone cold fear shivered through me. I knew all too well what Daren was capable of. "He'll come for you, I have no doubt. He's always been weak that way."

"He's a better man than you by far." My voice shook, but I lifted my chin while I slid my foot backwards, trying to get a little closer to the door. Maybe I could make a break for it. No one else had come over to us, though the guys across the room were watching our exchange with interest.

And Daren was overconfident. I was hoping that would be his downfall.

He clucked. "Now don't be so hasty in your judgments there, Princess. You haven't *had* me yet." He took a menacing step toward me, like a sinewy predator. "You don't know what a real man is like. But don't worry, I'll show you soon enough."

Not if I could help it.

I bolted for the door, but before I could open it, I was slammed against it, my whole body ringing from the impact. As I started to fall, Daren grabbed my arms. He held them behind me, hauled me to my feet, and spun me around so I was inches from his face.

"Let's try this again, you little bitch." His eyes were crazed, deep black pits. "I'm tired of waiting. Call. Him. Now."

"No." I shook my head. I was going down, I knew that, but I'd be damned if I was going to go down without a fight.

"I don't think you understand." He leaned in dangerously close, his breath hot on my face, his voice as sharp as the knife he slid under my chin. "This isn't a request. It's an order. You will tell me his fucking phone number."

"Fuck you. You're not getting a single digit from me." Involuntary shudders ran through my body, but I refused to let the prick see my fear. Not like that would change my fate. Still, I would not give him the satisfaction. I was only live bait to him, but at least I had that going for me. He needed me alive so he could get to Dare.

All I could think about was that I had to keep Dare far away from him. If my fate was already sealed and Daren was intent on killing me, so be it. But I was going to go down protecting the love of my life.

"String her up," he said, and smirked.

Two huge guys appeared out of nowhere, and wrapped thick rope around my wrists and feet. Every time I struggled, one of them smacked me across the face until my ears rang and the room swam. Then they lifted me up, slid my hands over the end of a metal bar above me and hung me there, my bound feet not even skimming the floor.

"Why are you protecting him?" Daren's blade hovered above my chest, teasing the hem of my camisole. "Hmm?"

"Because...I love him."

He laughed, then turned to one of his men and shook his head. "Did you hear that, Eddie? Someone loves the fucking failure. Ain't that something?"

"He's more of a man than you could ever hope to be." I spat the words at him, not caring if I pissed him off. He was going to kill me no matter what.

"You talk way too much for someone who's about to die." He backhanded me across the cheek, snapping my head to the side, filling my vision with blinding stars.

Eddie came closer, his eyes feasting on my body as if he were a starved man and I was an all-you-can-eat buffet.

"Let me have her for an hour, boss," he said stepping so close his rancid breath made me gag. "I'll show her *exactly* what she's been missing"

My eyes widened as I looked over at Daren, the hairs on the back of my neck rising.

Daren smiled again, and my blood froze, my breath stopped. He was considering letting the asshole have his way with me. Fucking monsters—both of them. My stomach knotted as Eddie licked his lips in anticipation.

But Daren shook his head, thank god. "No, I

want to keep her fresh. I want the boy to hear her first screams, see the first time. And the second. And the third. I want him to watch me cut into her and take her away from him piece-by-fucking-piece."

Disappointment intensified the ugly on Eddie's face. "Aw, come on. It's a waste to have such a pretty toy and not get any good use out of it before it goes to the dump. I promise not to break her." He grinned, his hand snaking out to me, aiming directly for the button of my jeans. "Not much, anyway," he added with a laugh.

Swinging my legs up and catching Eddie in the groin, I screamed, "NOOOO!"

He reeled, doubling over in pain even as he swung at me, his fist smashing painfully against my knee. "You little whore—"

"Enough!" Daren swore and shoved the blade at Eddie's throat. He nodded over his shoulder at the other thug. "Let's see if she'll talk this time while she's high. I want my bastard son here so I can kill this bitch already." He grabbed my chin and squeezed roughly. "Open wide, Princess." Then he stuffed a pill down my throat.

I was gasping for breath when he finally let go. Shuddering, I squeezed my eyes shut, trying to focus on breathing, knowing I had to stay strong for Dare.

Just a little longer. Just a little longer, then…

Then what?

If I didn't get away—and soon—I would be leaving this place in a body bag.

But in all reality, the longer I spent with Daren and his men, the better death was starting to look.

three
Dare

All I cared about was Ree.

Find Ree. Save Ree.

Hunt my father down before he killed her.

The police weren't going to do shit until they verified that she was actually in trouble—they'd made that clear when they'd questioned me at Rex's days ago.

It hadn't mattered that I'd pointed out all the evidence screaming that my father had taken her—her smashed phone on the studio floor, her partially packed bags, her purse still upstairs in her apartment, wallet untouched. She had no money, no credit cards, no ID.

It also hadn't mattered that I'd told them of his threats. That he'd already tried to blow her up in the gallery. They still moved at a snail's pace.

All I could think was find Ree. Save Ree.

When Rex's body had been covered by a sheet

and carried out on a stretcher in front of me, I'd lost it.

Rex was gone. Ree was gone. Who knew if she was even still alive? I had to get out of there and start looking for her.

Two exhausting long hours passed before the authorities were satisfied and I was finally released from questioning. But not before it became clear that Ree's kidnapping was not going to get the immediate attention it needed.

"She's an adult," the detective said. "Sometimes adults take off. It doesn't necessarily mean anything's happened to her."

Fuck it all—the police were going to be no help. At least not soon enough. Yeah, they'd eventually figure it out. Except Ree would be dead long before they decided she'd actually been kidnapped. I needed to find a way to spur them into action. Too bad the degenerate son of a criminal didn't have that kind of pull.

However, I knew someone who did.

The one person I never thought I'd ask for help—the root of this very problem, but also the only man who had enough power to make things happen—the mayor.

Ree's life was at stake, and there was no way in hell her dad could refuse to help.

Right?

I dialed his office, but as soon as I got through, his secretary brushed me off. "Mayor McKinley is in a meeting at the moment. Would you like to leave a message?"

"It's about his daughter." I threw a leg over my bike. "A matter of life and death."

"He'll get back to you soon." Then she hung up.

Jesus fucking Christ.

Desperate, I made another call.

"Archer Chase." He sounded formal and collected, and for a moment I was blinded with rage that anyone could be acting so normal when Ree had been taken. But then I realized he didn't know. Not yet.

"It's Dare Wilde." I paused, knowing this was going to be a kick in the nuts for him. "Ree's…"

"What's wrong?" he said. "Is she okay?"

"My fucking father has her, and I can't get anyone to do anything about it. Can't even get the mayor to pick up his phone. I need your he—"

"Meet me downtown. NOW." He gave me the address to his father's office where the mayor's meeting was being held. He'd get me in, no matter what.

Eighteen minutes later, we were riding the glass

elevator to the top floor. Storming past security and the front office staff, I followed him straight to the big corner office.

"Archer?" An older version of Archer—just as preppy, with grey-streaked blond hair and blue eyes—looked at us in surprise. His eyebrows' knit together in confusion.

The mayor shot me a glare dripping with distaste. "This is a private meet—"

"Ree's been taken," I said, fighting the urge to grab him by the lapels of his expensive designer suit and beat the living shit out of him. "Your daughter has been kidnapped by my father." I pointed at him. "You fucking started this, you have to help me end it. I'm going to find her, but I can't do it without your help."

Un-*fucking*-fortunately.

Whispers broke out throughout the room as the mayor's face blanched. But, by god, he actually leaped into action.

Someone was FINALLY taking this seriously.

"Get the Chief of police on the line." He nodded to the security guard, then turned to the man on his right. "Alert the media. I want this entire city looking for her. Within the next hour, Reagan's name must be on everyone's lips, her picture flashing on every television screen in the tri-state area."

Thank god.

Over the next several days, I was inundated with questions from reporters and the police. None of them had any clue where to find answers. Where to find Ree.

I sought out every contact of my father's I could find in the city, but got nothing out of them. No one knew anything. Or, more likely, no one was talking.

Fear consumed me, ate at me from the inside like acid spreading through my body. What no one seemed to understand—least of all the fucking mayor who spent more time posing for the press than speaking with the police—was that my father never played by anyone's rules.

The mayor called a daily press conference, and watching him playing the part of the concerned father made my blood boil. Because offstage he was much too calm and collected for a man who was on the verge of losing his child.

Behind me, two of the mayor's staff whispered excitedly.

"The girl's disappearance is guaranteed to help the mayor's campaign." The words, uttered by some silver-haired political flunky, made the hairs stand up on my neck. "He's a shoo-in for governor after all this press," he said to the lady next to him. "Let's be honest, all we need now is the dead body of a pretty blue-eyed, blonde girl, and he's sure to win."

I saw red. My entire body throbbed with rage. Before the man could utter another word, I'd turned and connected my fist with his dirty mouth.

"That's my girlfriend you're talking about, asshole! Ree is not some political pawn. Her life is not a fucking game!"

All I could think about was my father and his countless years of threats. Cameras descended on me, surrounding me as people hurried the mayor to safety.

If Ree died, he would never be safe from me. After I killed my father, I'd fucking hunt him down, too.

"Stop, Dare! Stop it!" Archer dragged me away from the now-bloodied man. Fuck, Abercrombie was stronger than he looked. He held out a hand toward the reporters. "Everything's okay—give him space!"

The crowd parted and a strange hush fell over the room. I looked straight into the biggest news station camera I saw and spoke directly to my father: "Listen closely, you sick piece of shit. It's me that you really want. Let her go and I'll come willingly. Just tell me where and when."

He'd get the message one way or another. I was sure of it.

And the second I was in front of him, I wouldn't hesitate to kill him.

I would find Ree. And I would save her.

four
Dare

"*FUCK!*" I slammed my phone down on the workbench in front of me. Paint bottles rattled in place as brushes rolled off the wooden surface and clattered to the floor. "Fuck, fuck, *fuck*."

Yet another dead end. Yet another old contact who swore up and down he hadn't heard from my dad.

Although I'd spent months ensuring my father had no way of finding me, I was now doing everything in my power to lead the bastard to me. I gave every fucking deadbeat my phone number to pass on to my dad just in case they happened to remember how to get in touch with him.

I had to get to Ree before it was too late. There was no time for any more press conferences, questions, or strategizing.

We had to do something NOW or we were

going to lose her. The clock on the wall was a ticking bomb, reminding me that time was running out. Each day, every hour, minute, and second, pulled her farther away from me.

Almost a week had passed since the kidnapping. Five days of silence and darkness. Over a hundred hours of no leads, no contact. More than seven thousand fucking minutes of not knowing a single thing.

Was she in pain? Was she afraid? Was she…alive?

Countless scenarios filled my head, each darker and more gruesome than the last. After all, this was my father we were talking about. A man without a heart, a monster devoid of a soul. I knew all too well what he was capable of, and the thought that he was anywhere near the woman I loved tortured me more than any of his beatings ever had.

But for Ree's sake—for our sake—I had to keep my shit together.

"Anything?" Archer's voice was low and tight.

I shook my head as he handed me another cup of coffee. "Nothing yet."

Tick-tock. Tick-tock.

"You've gotta get some rest, man. You have haven't slept since…" He looked away, unable to finish the sentence.

"And I won't sleep until she's found. Until she's safe. Until he's fucking dead." I took a swig, welcoming the burn of the hot liquid against my throat. Whatever pain Ree must be feeling right now, I wanted to feel it, too. "I'd give anything to trade places with her," I said, more to myself than my uninvited roommate.

"As would I," Archer replied quietly. His jaw was set and determination pulsed through his words.

"I know."

Ever since I'd called him, Archer had been there. Every step of the way. Day and night, he'd stayed glued to my side, setting up base on my couch.

Despite the intrusion, I couldn't bring myself to kick him out. Not when he kept me from going off the deep end.

He'd made himself and his resources available, drawing on his family's connections to help me track down my father's old contacts. It was hardly a surprise to find out how many things the Richie Riches of society had in common with the scumbag worms once we dug below the surface.

Still, we kept coming up empty handed.

Tick-tock. Tick-tock.

"GODDAMMIT!" I ripped the clock off the wall

and slammed it on the workbench. The cheap, plastic casing cracked in half, but the damn thing still kept ticking. Mocking me. Reminding me of what a failure I was.

I couldn't even keep my girl safe. I'd gotten her into this mess in the first place. If we hadn't been together…if she'd never met me…

"She should've been with you," I said, staring down at the fucking clock. "Someone…*normal*."

Archer scoffed. "Someone she doesn't love?" His eyes were ice hard, but there was no anger in his voice. "Reagan has always been the type to march to her own drum. She'd just spent too much time living life on mute until you came along. I might not be happy to admit it, but you're the best thing to ever happen to her." He nodded at a smiling portrait of Ree—the first one I'd done of her. *Real Ree.* "She chose you, Dare. Now man up and deal with it."

Easier said than done. Especially when guilt was ripping me up from inside. "She chose me to fuck up her life?"

"Some of us wish to have someone fuck up our lives." Archer's voice sounded distant. "Plus, you're not at fault. Reagan's father is."

Her father, the man who appeared to be riding out the media circus with hopes it would take him all the way to the fucking White House. The selfish asshole who was still spending more time with reporters than cops.

Before either of us could say anything more, Archer's phone rang.

"Detective Sutherland, hello," Archer said, and my heart froze in my throat as optimism flooded through me. Despite the fact that every other call we'd gotten thus far had been full of dead ends, I couldn't help but hope for some good news. "Uh-huh. Right. Yes."

"Yes?" I said, trying to read his face. "Yes, WHAT? Did they find her? Any leads?"

Archer shook his head and my heart plummeted. "Yes, I see. I'll pass on the news. Thank you, ma'am."

"No news yet," Archer said. "She just wanted to let us know that the police are doing everything they can."

I scoffed. "The police are a fucking joke. It wouldn't surprise me to find out my father has Detective Sutherland firmly in his back pocket. He always had a way with cops."

"We don't know—" Archer was cut off by another shrill ring. This time, it was my phone.

"You answer it." I shoved the device at him. "I'm going to explode if I hear another one of those motherfuckers lying about all the shit they're pretending to do."

I turned away from Archer, and ripped the batteries out of the clock. When he didn't make a sound, I glanced at him. His face was pale, his mouth hanging open.

"It's for you." He pressed his lips together and held out the phone. "It's him."

The floor seemed to shift under me. My stomach knotted as I grabbed the phone with one hand, steadying myself against the desk with the other.

This was it. The call I'd been waiting for. The call that meant Ree was still alive.

She fucking had to be.

"I see you got my message," I said, not waiting for him. My father was all about power—he craved and coveted control. Not this time. "Where is she?"

"Your little whore has caused quite a spectacle, hasn't she?" He barked the words out with a low, irritated growl. "If I'd known she was McKinley's girl I would've gone about this in an entirely different way. Demanded some money before I sliced into her tight, little body."

"If you've touched even a single hair on her head..." My voice and bravado wavered at the thought. No. I had to play his game. At least for the moment. "I'll do whatever you want if you just promise to let her go. I'll come willingly, just don't hurt her."

"Oh, you'll come anyway. You and I both know that." He laughed, then coughed like he was smoking up a storm. And the man only smoked that much when he was in the middle of a job. Fuck. "The bitch says she loves you. And it actually seems to be true." He tsked. "To think that somebody loves a loser like you. Did you know that she refused to give us your phone number? I cut into her pretty deep, but the cunt still wouldn't talk. She didn't even scream, though I'm willing to bet she will when you get here. She strikes me as the type who likes to perform in front of an audience."

"Don't you fucking touch her!" Panic and anger sliced through my chest. I saw blood. "I swear, I'll rip your head off if you hurt her!"

Archer's eyes widened.

"Where is she? Tell me where you're keeping her, you son-of-a-bitch! I'm coming to get her right now!"

Once again, my father laughed. "No, son. You're coming to watch her die. But at least you'll see her alive one last time."

Archer was in my ear. "We have to call the

cops, Dare!"

"Tell your little lackey, no cops. If I get even a whiff of pig, I won't hesitate to kill your girl before you get here. She'll be a puzzle you'll have to put back together piece by bloody fucking piece." He rattled off an address of an old shipyard in Jersey. "Just you. Come alone. Squeal to anyone and she dies before you get a chance to say goodbye."

My father hung up, and it took all my self-control not to stomp the shit out of my phone.

I looked at Archer. "I'm going after her."

"I'll call Detective Sutherland."

"No." I shook my head. "He said no cops or she dies."

"And we're supposed to listen to that?" He looked at me incredulously. "Are you fucking insane?"

"My father is," I said. "You don't know him, Archer. He never backs down. If he says he'll do it, he *will* do it. I refuse to risk her life."

"Then what are we going to do?"

"What he really wants is me. And I'm going to fucking give him what he wants. In spades. Then I'll bring her home."

Or die trying.

five
Reagan

"Oh, Prin-cess…" The strong smell of tobacco wafted over me as someone slapped my face. "Wake the fuck up."

The sting pierced the fuzziness of my mind, and I forced my heavy lids to lift, filling my vision with bright, burning light. Nothing looked familiar. Had I been out partying? I couldn't remember where I was or who I'd been with. And, fuck, every square inch of me was in pain.

"We're going to have a visitor today." A blurry mouth was an inch away from my nose, scarred lips turned up in a malicious sneer. The man kept coming in and out of focus, as if he was a prop on some hellish carnival ride I was stuck on. "Can you guess who's coming to watch you die?"

Dare. Despite my drugged haze, he was always the first thought in my mind. Dare, Dare, Dare. Always Dare.

But why was he coming to watch me die? Was I sick?

And then clarity returned like a cold, cruel wind, blowing the memories of the past few days through my mind. Daren Wilde's face was now fully in focus, and my body instinctively tensed, preparing for the first blow.

The first one was always the worst. No matter how much I braced myself for it, the intensity of the pain took my breath away. I should have been used to it by now, but I was starting to think that maybe there were some things in this world that you simply could not get used to.

At least I knew that when it was all over, they'd drug me again, and I'd have the bliss of oblivion to take away the pain. Blood and drugs. That had become my world over the past few days as Daren tried to get me to give up Dare's phone number.

I hadn't caved, had I?

No. I was sure of it. But Dare was coming, which meant his father had gotten to him.

Dare was in danger, and I'd failed to protect him. Fuck.

I tried to scream, to swear at the monster in front of me, but no sound came out. Gritting my teeth, I bit down on the cloth between my lips, groaning in frustration as a few traitorous tears slipped down my cheeks.

Daren shook his head. "No, no, Princess," he said. "Save the crying for *after* he arrives. It'll be much more heart-wrenching that way." He smirked. "Don't worry, you won't have to wait long. The ungrateful bastard should be here any minute now." He slowly undid my gag. "I'm warning you now that any screaming will only force me to drug you again. And you really, really need to be awake for this part of the show. It'll be all the more fun."

Shouts exploded outside, and Daren's head turned toward the sounds. Something crashed into the wall, and I swore I could hear the sickening sound of fists hitting flesh.

Daren turned back to me, a deadly grin on his face. "Looks like he's already here." He licked his lips. "Once they get him tied down, they'll bring him in to me."

So he could kill Dare?

Not if I had anything to say about it.

Using all my strength, I jerked forward, slamming my head into his face as I yelled, "Run, Dare! Get out of here!"

Daren reared back, howling, blood gushing out of his nose. "Jesus fucking Christ! You broke my fucking nose!"

Clutching his face with both hands, he lifted one black-booted foot and kicked me in the chest, sending me tumbling over backwards in the chair I was tied to. I felt bones crunch as my weight came down on my hands trapped behind me.

Pain shot up my arms and I groaned.

"You fucking bitch." He pulled out his knife, grabbed hold of my right arm, and pulled. The pain in my wrist was excruciating, and I screamed as he wrenched me and the chair back up. "I should just kill you right now."

He walked around behind me, and I closed my eyes, praying he'd make it quick, but knowing that wasn't the least bit likely. I tried to hold Dare in my mind and heart, warm myself with his love so my last thought would be of him and only him. I heard Daren move swiftly, braced myself for the blow as stale air swished around us, but felt the knife slice between my hands, and my arms swung free.

My right hand throbbed and I couldn't move my fingers, but I didn't have time to do anything except gasp in surprise at my freedom before he grabbed me by the hair and lifted me to my feet.

"LET HER GO!"

No, no, no. He wasn't supposed to come in

here.

My chest tore in half at the sight of Dare, his complexion pale, dark circles surrounding his sunken eyes. Bruises were forming on his face, his lip was busted, and his knuckles were bleeding, but he was otherwise none the worse for wear.

I blinked back tears. I'd been wishing and praying to see him one last time, but now that he was standing in front of me, horror washed over me and all I could think was that he'd just sealed his own fate.

His death.

"And the prodigal rat returns." Daren spat, pulled his gun out of the back of his pants, and pointed it at Dare. "Nice of you to finally join us." He waved his gun toward the door. "Though you were supposed to have an escort."

"I got rid of them," Dare said coolly. "It's just you and me now. Let Ree go."

"*Dare…*" I shook my head. If he thought there was even a chance his father was going to just let me walk out of here after all this, he was insane. I knew better. He *had* to know better after a lifetime spent in this monster's shadow.

"Let Ree go," he said again, his eyes glued to mine. "I'm here. Take me, do whatever you want to me, just release her."

Daren tutted. "That would be too easy, wouldn't it? I want you to suffer the way you've made me suffer all these years. My wife, my kids, my business—you've murdered them all. I had to watch from behind bars as everything of mine was ripped away. All because I let you in, you ungrateful, selfish bastard."

"That was all your own doing," Dare said. "Your greed cost you your business. And you lost your family because you're a malicious, psychotic son-of-a-bitch."

"Haven't you learned yet that there are consequences for talking back to your father?" Daren backhanded me with his pistol, and Dare surged forward but froze as soon as his father trained the gun on him again.

"I will fucking kill you if you hurt her again." Dare's eyes blazed, his whole body tensed as if he might pounce. But I hoped to god he wouldn't. Not with that gun pointing right at his heart. "I will rip you to shreds, piece by little piece."

"Funny, that's exactly what I was planning to do to your little whore." Daren yanked me back against him, and my skin crawled at the feel of his hot breath on my neck. "Though maybe I should just shoot you instead." I could almost hear the slow malevolent grin spread across his face. "As for you, Princess, I'll get your daddy to set me up with a big, fat reward. I'll be set for life, free to start over wherever the fuck I want. I hear California is the place to be these days."

My eyes traveled down his right arm to the gun in his hand. It was close enough that I could reach it. I glanced at Dare, his gaze bore into me and he shook his head just slightly. But it was our only chance. Daren's finger was poised to squeeze, if I didn't do something now, it might be too late.

And I was not going to be too late to save Dare.

With all of my might, I stomped on Daren's boot and he lost his grip on my hair. I lunged for his gun, but he swung it at me, aiming right at my head.

"NO!" Dare yelled, thrust his palms forward as if that might stop his father. "It's me you want. Just let her go. I'll stay. You have my word."

"*Your* word?" His father laughed, his eyes bright with insanity. "Your fucking word means nothing. You snitched me out before, you little shit. You think I don't know that? You think I don't know exactly *who* was responsible for me going to jail?"

Dare shook his head. "You did that yourself. They caught you because you took the time to put me in the hospital."

Daren's gaze was fixed on his son, his eyes

bugging out, his expression incredulous. I slid one foot toward Dare and ever so slowly started to shift my weight toward him.

But as soon as I'd begun to move, Daren's eyes were back on me. "You fucking move a muscle again and I will fucking shoot you."

"Come on. You've got to let her go. You can't keep track of both of us. And there's no one here to help you." Dare took a step forward, and Daren's trigger finger started to squeeze. "NO! IT'S *ME* YOU WANT."

Daren's eyes flicked to Dare, and he considered him for a brief moment. "You know what? You're right. It's *you* I want. It's *you* I want to see suffer. It's *you* I want to have watching while I take away the woman you love. It's *you* I want to bring to your knees. And I'm going to do that right now."

He suddenly swung his arm toward Dare, aiming at his legs, his finger starting to squeeze the trigger.

And the world practically stopped, everything happening as if in slow motion.

I launched myself forward, not thinking about what I was doing, my only impulse to save the man I loved. I was flying through the air when an ear-splitting BANG rang out, reverberating through my body. Then something stung my stomach, and I was falling to the hard cold floor.

I screamed as agony unlike any other I'd ever felt ripped through me. The entire side of my body felt engulfed in flames.

Darkness closed in on me as I lifted my head to see if Dare was okay. To see if he'd been shot. But he was a blur. Fear and rage contorted his face as he hurled himself at his father. They were a tangle of fists and blows, wrestling for control of the gun between them.

Wet warmth seeped through my fingers as my eyes started to close, and the last thing I heard was the sound of Daren's gun going off.

Then everything went black.

six
Reagan

I was trapped in a murky, dark dream, lost in a fog. Shivering. So very cold. My ears were ringing, my limbs immobile, and the intense pressure in my head made me feel as if I was submerged under water.

Maybe I was drowning.

Images filtered through the haze of my mind— Dare fighting with his dad, a gun going off, and then…nothing. Oh, god. What if he'd been killed? I had to get out of here. I had to claw my way to the surface.

"No, no, noooo!" My throat was raw, my cries raspy. "NO!" Tangles of tubes imprisoned me, my right hand couldn't move, and a fast, loud beeping sound was going off like a warning bell. "Dare! Oh, god…no." I tried to break free.

My body screamed in protest.

"Ree." The smooth, low sound of his voice

went straight to my pounding heart, easing my panic into calm. "Hey, easy. *Easy.*" Blinking furiously, I forced the world—and Dare's bruised face—into focus. He stood next to me, his hands stilling my arms. "It's okay, baby."

"You're alive." Tears flowed from my eyes as my heart welled with relief. My throat tightened and I had to swallow several times before I could speak again. His own eyes looked glassy as he gazed at me and nodded.

"You are, too."

I glanced around the room. "I'm in the hospital?"

He nodded. "We really gotta stop meeting like this," he said with a smile.

Oh, god. He was alive. We were *both* alive. I wanted to laugh. I wanted to kiss him.

I wanted to know that this was real.

"You're okay?" I needed to hear him say it out loud. "This isn't a dream? Please tell me this isn't a dream."

Dare leaned closer, pressing his warm lips to my cool forehead. "It's not a dream."

"What happened?"

He pulled back and gazed down at me. The circles around his eyes were even darker now. He seemed so…drained. Yet the smile still clung to his lips.

"I got you back," he said softly. "That's what happened." He looked over to the machine next to my bed. "But you…" He trailed off and pressed his lips together as he swallowed hard. "You saved my life, Ree. You…" He shook his head, unable to speak for a moment. When he did, his voice was tight. "You saved me."

I reached up and touched his face with my left hand. He leaned into my palm, stubble scratching my skin, his tender lips brushing against it. He was all sorts of hard and soft. And real. He was really, really REAL.

"I couldn't let him hurt you anymore," I said. "It was instinct."

"It was crazy," Dare said. But he would've done the same for me. Hell, he already had. Countless times. He'd saved my life over and over again. "You scared me to death." Then he laughed at his choice of words. "Shit. No pun intended." He kissed my forehead again, ever so softly making his way down my nose to my lips. "I'm so glad you're okay. I don't know what I would have done if you'd…"

"I know. Me, too." I took a deep, shaky breath and tried to sit up, but my side felt like it was on fire. I gasped at the pain. Fuck, this hurt.

Dare raised my bed and gently shifted another pillow behind me, so I was half-sitting. "The bullet went straight through your phoenix's heart." He gently placed his hand on the upper part of my right thigh. "Thankfully it went clean through and out the other side."

"What about your dad?" I said, shuddering at the mere thought of him, but I had to know. "Is he…?"

"He's dead."

Relief washed over me, though it didn't feel real. It didn't make me feel safe. It didn't make me feel better.

"Oh, my god. What about Rex? He was trying to protect me, Dare…and he…Daren shot…"

Agony sliced across Dare's beautiful face, his eyes grew watery, and my heart stopped.

No. Oh, please no. "Oh, my god, Dare. I'm so…he can't be…" A sob escaped my lips as tears filled my eyes again.

"Rex is…gone." He leaned forward, wrapped his arms around me, and we held onto each other as we cried.

In so many ways, Rex had brought us together and kept us together…even when we were apart. That he was…oh, god, the pain in my heart was worse that the wound in my side.

Rex was gone. Dead. And he'd died because of me.

Dare saw the look on my face, felt the guilt scorching my insides. "Don't go there, Ree," he whispered hoarsely. "It wasn't your fault. It was mine." He took a deep breath. "Can you ever forgive me?"

"Forgive you for what?"

"For everything. For what my father did, for letting you get hurt, for Rex, for—"

"Dare, *no*." I pressed a finger to his lips. "Don't. I refuse to lie here and listen to you apologize for what that monster did. You weren't responsible for any of it."

"But—"

"And your love was the one thing—the ONLY thing—that kept me going through all the pain. It kept my heart beating. So don't apologize for saving me."

"You're the one who saved me." He shook his head. "You've always saved me. From the moment I met you and every minute since." He picked up my left hand, held it gently in his, rubbing his thumb in circles over my skin. "I want to color your world, Ree. I want to be the source of your laughter, to inspire your smiles, to share in all the good that's yet to come." He leaned back in the chair and fished something out of his jacket pocket.

A small blue velvet box.

Oh. My. God.

"I don't ever want us apart again. My heart broke at the thought of losing you. I can't bear to go through that ever again. I want to spend the rest of my life with you." He opened the box to reveal a small, antique silver ring with the most beautiful, brilliant sapphire stone set in the middle of it. "We are two parts of a whole," he said. "We always have been. Say you'll be my other half forever, Ree."

"Yes." I nodded. My head felt like it weighed a freaking ton, but I didn't care. "Yes, yes, yes. Forever and then some."

Exhaling sharply, he slid the ring on my finger and then claimed my mouth with his. His tongue entwined with mine, sending tingles down my spine. My heart was on a sprint and my head was on a tilt-a-whirl. The kiss seemed like it was going to go on forever—not that I was complaining—but he pulled away slightly to let me catch my breath. His lips were still so close to mine, his fingers still interlocked with my own, and his eyes refused to let me go.

The look he gave me warmed every part of my

body, delving into my soul and spreading through me like warm, rich chocolate. It was a look from a best friend. A lover. A soul mate. A partner in all the good and the bad.

It held a promise that, from now on, our world was going to be filled with only happiness, laughter, and love. We were going to live the rest of our lives in bright, vibrant color.

We were way overdue.

seven
Dare

We stood in front of Rex's gravestone, and all I could think about was the fact that the drab, gray marble wasn't worthy of the man nor his memory. Even the "Beloved Friend and Father" inscription seemed like it wasn't doing enough, wasn't saying everything it should. Everything I wanted people to know about Rex.

He'd saved me. Plain and simple.

Not only had he been the most brilliant artist of his time, he'd been the most generous person I knew. He'd taken me in when he should have booted me out the door. He'd given me a second chance after I'd fucked up the first.

He'd loved me like my own father never had— like a son.

And the gaping hole he'd left in my life hurt like hell.

"Aw, fuck, Ree," I said. The late November

wind cut across my skin, stinging my face, chilling me to the bone. I wiped my eyes with the back of my hand, and pulled her closer into me. If it hadn't been for her, my heart would be completely empty. Missing Rex.

"I know," she said as she pressed her cheek into my leather jacket. "Me, too."

No matter how firmly I hugged her or how hard I kissed her, I felt like we still couldn't be close enough. Three weeks had passed since I'd gotten her back, but I still couldn't let her out of my sight.

For the first time in my life, I had everything I wanted. Well, almost everything. But it had come at a steep price. For us both.

"What are we going to do with all of Rex's stuff?" Ree bit down on her lip and glanced up at me. "We can't just keep ignoring the fact that you've inherited his estate. Things have to be taken care of…" Her eyes glistened with tears. "We have to do right by him, Dare."

"I don't want his money," I said immediately. "It's not right."

Two weeks ago, mere days after burying him, his attorney had called to tell me that Rex had left everything to me in his will. Money, paintings, even his house. He had no other family, and had listed me as his sole beneficiary.

Having led a frugal, reclusive life, he'd accumulated an impressive amount of savings. If I chose to keep the money, Ree and I were guaranteed an easy ride for the rest of our lives.

A ride that would be funded by blood money.

"I can't, Ree…"

"I know. I can't either." She was quiet for a while, then said, "So we won't."

I looked over at her in surprise. "You really mean that?"

She nodded. "We don't need that money." We both knew that was a big, fat lie. She'd severed all financial ties with her parents months ago, and I'd lost most of my work in the explosion at La Période Bleue. To say that we were broke was an understatement.

Still…

"I just can't stand to profit from this," I said. "It would feel too much like I was celebrating his death."

She looked down at the flowers laid out on the frozen earth—piles of them from friends, colleagues, and fans—and smiled softly. "Then what about celebrating his life instead? What if, instead of keeping the money, we did something with it in Rex's honor? Something that celebrates the mark he left behind, both in the art world and in our hearts."

I took a deep breath, filling my lungs with crisp, winter air. When I was at my lowest, Rex had been the only one to believe in me. Not only that, but he'd also supported my work when no one else would. By the time I got out of juvie, many people had written me off completely. And those who hadn't only wanted me to be Daren Junior.

Rex had steered me onto the right path, never doubting that I would get my act together. His faith in me had made me want to be better, do better. To be more like him.

And I suddenly knew exactly what we could do with the money to achieve that.

"What do you think about creating a scholarship fund in Rex's name to an art school?" I said. "Something to help underprivileged kids looking to make a positive change in their lives, a transition in the right direction."

Ree's face lit up. "It's perfect. I know Rex would approve." She rose up on her tiptoes and brushed her lips against my cheek. "He'd be so proud. It will be a celebration of the two of you as a team."

The two of you. Those words stung.

Rex and Dare. Never again.

"But I need more time to decide what to do about the townhouse," I said. "Rex lived there for over thirty years."

"We don't have to rush it." Ree gave me a reassuring squeeze. "There's time, Dare."

While I couldn't part with the place, there was also no way in hell I could live there. And I knew with certainty that Ree couldn't either. Not after everything that had happened within those walls.

"As for his art…" I stiffened. Fuck, this hurt. "I can't sell his paintings." They were him. The only tangible thing I had left of Rex. The money and the house were mere objects, but those paintings were his fucking soul.

Ree shook her head. "We'll keep them forever. When you're ready, we can adorn our entire house with his work. And when I have my own gallery one day, I'll have monthly exhibits dedicated to him." Her mouth quirked up in a small smile. "Don't worry, I'll try to leave room on my walls for some Wildes, too."

eight
Dare

I felt Rex's presence as Ree and I worked to pack up his house over the next week. He was everywhere—and nowhere—all at once.

"Dare, come in! Show me your latest work. I want to see how you've grown."

I saw him in front of the old gas stove where he taught me to cook so I could make sure the twins wouldn't go hungry. His laughter echoed in the TV room that was riddled with a mountain of those damn Smothers Brothers tapes he loved so much. How he was able to watch the same episode over and over again, and *still* find something to laugh about had always baffled me. As did the fact that he refused to switch to DVDs when most of the modern world got rid of their VCRs.

"Why would I need something new? I already have everything I could wish for."

The house smelled of his faint, woodsy cologne. It even sighed and groaned every so often as if it, too, was missing him. Hell, his spirit even bloomed in the now-withered and frost-covered vegetable patch he kept in his tiny yard.

But, most of all, Rex's presence filled his studio. I hadn't been able to even pick up my own brushes since he'd died, and the thought of packing his away killed me. It took me the full week to actually work up the strength to go in there. Ree was my rock, diligently cleaning the room and protecting as many canvases as she could from dust, but in the end I knew I wouldn't be at peace until I faced the room head-on.

"This is my sacred space, Dare. When you invite someone into your studio, you invite them into your life."

My chest constricted the moment I crossed the threshold, my throat closing around the sob that threatened to escape. I walked quietly around the perimeter of the room, afraid to disturb anything. Sunshine filtered through a stained glass piece hanging in one of his windows, coating the hardwood floor in color.

"Don't be afraid of color. That's like being afraid of life! How can anyone be afraid of something so beautiful, so perfect?"

The very first day I'd snuck into the studio

through the open back door, I'd been six years old. My dad had been angry. And high. I'd sought refuge from his wrath at Rex's. Having slipped inside unnoticed, I was struck by the vibrant hues pulsing through the room. It was as if even the air was saturated with every shade, and I breathed it in like I'd been holding my breath all my life.

Color was everywhere. On the walls, on the dusty desk by the window, on big, white canvases. When Rex found me covered in paint and blasting his paintbrushes off into space, he hadn't gotten angry like my father would have.

No, Rex had laughed. And invited me to stay.

In his studio, and in his life.

He'd held out a paintbrush and nodded toward his canvas. "You wanna give it a try? Here. Help me finish off this wing."

My eyes widened. "You want ME to work on YOUR picture? What if I make a mistake?"

He shot me a big, lopsided grin. "Let's hope you do. Mistakes are the best way to learn."

With a shaky hand, I dipped my brush in paint and carefully added some bright red to the golden wing. It took a few slow strokes, but it made me feel better. Made me forget about my dad and that new bruise under my mom's eye.

Rex smiled wide as he watched me work. The

creature was starting to look like it was burning with light and power. I loved it.

"This dragon is going to look super cool when I'm done with it."

He laughed. "It's a phoenix," he'd said. "The strongest, most majestic creature."

"What? No. Everyone knows that dragons are the most powerful things in the world!" I couldn't believe he didn't know that. "They breathe fire and can kill everyone. That's why my dad has a tattoo of a dragon on his back."

Rex opened his mouth, but then quickly pressed his lips together. "Real power isn't measured by the fire you breathe nor the pile of ashes you leave behind, Dare," he said slowly. "It's about the hope you inspire."

Rex had inspired hope in me. Hope that my life could be better, that I could do better, that I could change my path, be proud of who I was and what I did. Rex *was* hope. The one thing I'd needed more than anything else back then.

Rex had been the first to call me Dare. And it stuck from day one. I left Daren behind, in so many ways, after I met him.

"FUCK!" I smashed my fist into the table now, crushing tubes of paint the way the pain in the middle of my chest was crushing me. The sticky substance splattered everywhere. My other fist followed. Hard. "Fuck, fuck, *fuck*!"

I didn't care that I was spilling paint that would never be used again or that my knuckles hurt like shit. I let loose all the rage I'd been bottling up for weeks as I was overwhelmed by Rex's loss.

Punch.

Punch.

Punch.

I didn't stop pounding. Not even when my hands were stinging and covered in a dark brown mess. Not even when my knuckles were raw and red. Not even when the tears came or when my knees buckled and I crashed to the floor.

Still, I went on punching.

My thighs. The floor.

Eventually the rage ebbed, and I was left with this hollow, numb feeling inside.

But nothing took away the pain.

nine
Reagan

Oh, god. Walking into Rex's studio, I saw him. Really, truly saw him.

All paint and pain and passion.

It shattered me. I felt Dare's agony to the very core of my being, pulsing painfully hard with every moment Rex was gone. I didn't say a word as I rushed across the room and wrapped myself around him, wishing I could somehow funnel the pain away.

His voice sounded soaked with tears. "Fuck…this hurts, Ree. I can't…"

"I know, baby." I murmured into his hair. "I know."

Color had fully claimed him, streaking his face, splattering his jeans, covering his hands and arms. Even his disheveled hair was tipped with bright tones as if he'd tugged at the strands.

He was color—a living, breathing piece of

artwork.

But the look he was giving me was filled with only darkness.

I gripped his face, forcing him to look at me, and pressed my lips against his. "Don't let him win, Dare. We can't let him win. Rex wouldn't want that."

"Rex is dead." He fisted my sweater so tightly the hem lifted off my stomach, exposing the still healing scar. "And there's nothing I can do to bring him back." His shoulders shook. His entire body was quaking against mine as he wrapped his arms around me. "Why does it have to hurt so fucking much?"

"Because you loved him so much." A lump formed in my throat, and I hugged his head to my chest, pressing kisses against his forehead. "It hurts because you loved him."

My fingers wove through his hair, and I kept kissing him, willing my touch to relieve his pain, to bring light back into his darkness. His breathing calmed and changed as I covered his face with kisses, and when my lips found his again, his fingers dug into my waist, pulling me closer. His lips met mine, hard and hungry, leaving me breathless as his darkness morphed into intense need.

Dare's tongue delved inside me, greedy and demanding, possessing my mouth almost like he was staking his claim all over again. The kiss was the lovechild of lust and passion, want and need. It burned through me, dispersing a wildfire of tremors down my body, igniting sensations that had been dormant for far too long.

For the past month, as I recovered from my injuries, things between the two of us had been very...*gentle*. Dare had been so intent on not causing me any more pain, he'd limited himself to sweet kisses and soft embraces.

But this moment was the exact opposite of that. It was fiery and hot. Unrelenting. Raw. Pulsing with life. Dare's desire vibrated through me, mingling with my own.

I wanted more. Closer. Harder.

I was ready, and I needed him as much as he needed me.

His name was a string of pleas on my lips, and he drank every one of them, lapping up my words with his tongue, giving me exactly what I wanted.

Hands brushing through my hair, he tugged gently on the locks before gliding his fingers over my back to my sides. He held on tight and pulled me onto his lap, shifting my peasant skirt up so he could lock my legs around his waist, bringing me even closer into his warmth, his lips never leaving my body.

Kissing down my neck, he slipped one hand under my sweater and glided his palm over my stomach to cup my breast, caressing my nipple over the fabric of my bra.

"I love you so fucking much," he said into my lips, the deep, husky words making me tremor with longing. Tugging the sweater over my head, he blazed a trail of kisses down my neck and collarbone. "And, god, I've missed you." He unclasped my bra and caressed every inch of my breast with his mouth, teasing my nipples to tight peaks with his tongue and teeth.

Arching my back, I pushed against him and moaned for more.

Always more when it came to Dare.

"I get so lost in you." My words were low and raspy.

"God, Ree." He was panting hard, his chest heaving, his breath hot against my ear as he whispered, "I want to spend the rest of my life losing myself in you. Just like this."

He kissed every inch of my breasts and stomach, nibbled on my collarbone. His lips were setting off fireworks in places I had no idea could even feel this kind of thrill from a simple touch.

But this wasn't just a simple touch from any guy.

This was Dare.

Unrestrained. Unbridled. Untamed.

The other half of my heart. My always and forever.

I slid my fingers along the waistband of his jeans, unbuttoning them, ripping his zipper down. Before I could take him in my hands, though, he trapped my wrist.

"Not here." He nodded at a row of Rex's paintings, placing his arms under me and pulling us up to a standing position. "The apartment. Upstairs."

We somehow made it up the steep stairs to my—and Dare's—old place without detangling our limbs or lips. Crashing into walls, bumping against furniture, we kissed our way to the bedroom.

He released me and peeled off his shirt. With his hands above his head, his muscles tightened, cutting across his skin so sharply he looked dangerous to the touch. But I didn't hesitate in reaching out and trailing my fingers across his firm abs. I loved the feel of his body—the combination of hard muscle and soft skin always made me weak in the knees.

And wet. A pulse grew between my thighs as I touched him, the anticipation of feeling him moving inside me fueling it even further. Every single part of me was desperate to feel him pressed against my body. When I delved lower, tracing the sharp muscles that dipped into his jeans, he groaned and pressed himself against my hand.

"You're covered in paint." I laughed, my lips against his chest, tasting him, savoring him.

Dare lowered his mouth to my ear. "Then how about a nice, hot, dirty shower?"

"A *dirty* shower?" My cheeks were flushed with arousal, my lips puffy.

"Oh, yes. A filthy one," he murmured, then claimed my lips again, his mouth and tongue inspiring all sorts of naughty thoughts to flit through my mind. "I need you so fucking bad." The edge in his voice made me shudder in anticipation. "Right now, right here."

Losing myself in the heated kiss, I grabbed his hand and brought it down between my legs to show him how much I needed him too.

Almost a month without naked Dare made for a very impatient, horny Ree.

His fingers slid inside my panties, grazing my throb, making me moan into his mouth as they slipped inside.

"Jesus, Ree." He breathed the words, and picked me up, carrying me into the bathroom.

The tiles he set me down on were cold against my feet, but I barely noticed. My entire body was ablaze with his touch.

He turned on the shower and looked back at me, the sweetest, naughtiest grin igniting his sharp features. One that went both to my wild, hammering heart and other, more tingly parts that were clamoring for attention.

My skirt and underwear were down my legs and off my body within seconds. Dare's jeans followed. He adjusted the water temperature and pulled me into the shower with him.

The hot water made his skin slick and smooth, and my hands couldn't get enough of him. I wanted to touch him everywhere, feel every inch of his body against mine.

"Let me wash you," he said, his hands already lathering up with the soap I'd left behind all those weeks ago.

I arched an eyebrow. "I thought this was supposed to be a dirty shower."

"Oh, it will be. But want I to get my hands on you first. I want to feel all of you, wet and slippery like this. I want to tease you before making you beg for the dirty."

Oh, god. Yes, please.

His hands felt so good as they slid up my arms, over my shoulders and breasts, trailing down my stomach, careful to avoid my wound. I couldn't stifle my moans when he worked his way lower, slipping his fingers between my legs, teasing my opening with a preview of what was to come. He kissed my neck, sucking on my wild pulse, one thumb circling my clit as his other hand went back up to my breast to lightly pinch my nipple.

"You have to let me have a turn," I said between raspy breaths. "Please."

But when I tried to wash him in return, to satisfy my craving to feel him, he lost all ability to behave. He shut his eyes and leaned his head back, allowing me to lather his body for less than a minute before grasping my wrists and pushing himself against me. His erection pressed into my stomach as he trapped me between a rock-hard slab of muscles and a cold, wet wall.

"Fuck it, Ree. I can't wait anymore. I need you now. I want to take you hard." He parted my thighs with his knee and slid his hand up the inside of my leg, toward my pulsing core. Caressing my folds, he brushed the tip of his finger over my clit, then plunged inside. "I want to make you feel just how much I fucking love you. From inside out."

Groaning at the sudden invasion and the welcomed pleasure it brought, I tightened around him and pushed my hips forward in an attempt to bring him even deeper. He obeyed, giving me another finger at the same time as his lips closed around the peak of my breast, sucking my nipple into his warm mouth.

Oh, god…I'd missed this so much. I'd missed *him* so much.

"More, Dare. More of you, *please*."

"You're so fucking tight, baby." His voice was barely audible over the sound of the shower as the spray beat against our skin, but the lust throbbing through it was undeniable. "I don't think I'll be able to restrain myself for long hearing you beg like that, knowing how deliciously tight and wet you are right now."

He moved his fingers inside me, first slowly, testing out my limits, but then with increased speed and intensity. In and out. Deeper and faster. Just the way I needed it.

The motion threatened to bring me over the edge in record time. When he rubbed his thumb over my clit, I cried out his name.

"I'm going to come," I said, hooking my leg

around his waist and bringing his hardness against my opening. "But I want to come with you inside me. Please, Dare. Please don't hold back."

His mouth came down on mine, hard and rough, and he pulled my leg higher up, parting my thighs, bearing me to him as he throbbed against me.

"You have no idea how badly I needed to hear that." With those words, he thrust his hips forward, burying himself deep into me.

Spreading me. Filling me. Completing me.

I gasped, then moaned, so fucking pleased with how he felt inside. I'd been craving this, yearning for him, desperate to be devoured by his love.

Everything he did told me just how much this moment meant to him, too. It was in the way he rocked his hips and the urgency with which he dug his fingers into my skin as if he couldn't get enough contact. It flowed through the things that surged from his mouth between kisses, painting me with the color of his words: *so perfect, so beautiful, so mine.*

Every muscle on his body was tensed as he pumped into me, his thighs flexed and his legs holding up our weight. Our kisses were frantic. We breathed for each other, into each other, with each other—existing as one. This moment was what raw, real love was all about. It wasn't perfect. It was carnal, painful, beautiful, and even a little desperate.

We weren't making love. We weren't fucking.

We'd reached a completely different plane.

For the first time ever, we really, truly were *one*.

ten
Reagan

When I peered through the peephole of our apartment a week later, the last people I expected to be on the other side were my parents. I hadn't seen them since the day Dare had found me.

I'd been groggy when my father had burst into my hospital room with a gaggle of reporters clamoring to capture the moment of reunion between a concerned father and his poor, victimized daughter. My mother stood to one side, a handkerchief in her hand and tears almost in her eyes.

It was the photo op of the century for them.

I'd been too out of it to react, but Dare hadn't. He'd thrown the reporters out amidst a flurry of flashes going off, and then stayed by my side during the subsequent awkward visit. Since then, my parents had been too busy winning and then celebrating my father's election, and I'd ignored every one of their calls for appearing at press conferences.

And yet, here they stood, looking incredibly uncomfortable and out of place. My mother kept throwing glances toward the street, eyeing the few neighborhood kids hanging around as if she expected them to do something "undesirable" at any moment.

But there were much worse things in this world, I knew all too well.

The sheer stupidity of the situation should have made me laugh, but I was too stunned by their presence to do anything but open the door and gape at them.

"Honestly, Reagan," my mother said, her hand patting her hair as she turned to look behind her one more time. "It is proper to invite people in when you answer the door. You were not raised by wolves."

"Nope. More like snakes." I held the door open wider to usher them inside.

"What?" Her eyes widened as she scurried into the seeming safety of the apartment.

Safety was relative, I'd learned. I was still having trouble feeling safe anywhere if I allowed myself to think about it. So I didn't. As much as possible.

When Dare and I were together, I felt fine.

Especially at home here. The problem was going out. I felt exposed, vulnerable, like a walking target. No matter how many times I reminded myself that Daren was dead and gone, I still couldn't shake the feeling that danger was lurking around every corner.

Shit happened. And if it had happened once, it could happen again.

"Reagan." My father nodded as he passed. Things had been frosty between us ever since I'd trumped him with Stanzi, but he no longer treated me like I was his own personal Doormat Barbie. We both knew that he couldn't manipulate me into doing whatever he asked anymore. I'd more than earned his respect—I'd blackmailed him into giving it to me. And I liked that feeling more than I'd expected.

Perched on the sofa a few minutes later, they both looked wildly out of place on our well-worn brown leather couch. My mother even had the audacity to wipe the seat off before she slowly lowered herself onto it, only after taking the time to scrutinize the room with a distasteful, icy glare, of course.

I tried to see the apartment through her eyes, but all I saw was Dare. Everywhere. He was color, vibrant and true, and he was splashed all over the walls—his paintings, Rex's, and other artists he'd collected over the past several years. I loved this place so much. It was the polar opposite of my parents' house—I was sure their senses must have been overwhelmed. Considering they viewed the world in black, white, and the multitudes of grays in between, I wasn't sure if they still even had the ability to see in color, to feel warmth.

I started shaking my head as I looked at them, wondering why in the world they were actually here, thanking god Dare was out—he didn't need to be subjected to their bullshit.

"So," I said, after I'd carefully sunk into the overstuffed armchair across from them. Even though my wound had healed, the ghost of pain from those first few excruciating days haunted me. And so I still moved with caution. "To what do I owe this…pleasure?"

It was an incredible stretch calling their visit that, but what the hell. My head ached, my stomach felt tight and hard, and I was dying to swallow something just to take the edge off.

My pain pills were gone, and the drugs Dare's dad had pumped through me were completely out of my system, but still I felt the craving like a deep, dark itch. An itch there was only one way to scratch.

No, I couldn't think like that. Not again. Not anymore.

I swallowed the longing, shut out the thirst, and made a mental note to call my sponsor after my parents left.

One moment at a time, I reminded myself. I would get back to where I'd been.

I'd done it once, I'd do it again.

My father cleared his throat. "Before I head up to Albany in January, I was hoping we could settle things with you."

Frowning, I said, "Settle things?"

"Harvard." I opened my mouth to tell him exactly where he could stick law school, but he held up his hands. "Just listen to me for a moment. I underestimated you, I admit it."

"Yes, you did."

"And I will not make that mistake a second time." He leaned forward, rested his elbows on his knees. "I want you on my team, Reagan. I need a brilliant mind like yours working for me...challenging me." He sighed. "I have surrounded myself with people who tell me what I want to hear. I need someone who will tell me when I'm wrong. Like you." I began shaking my head, but he held up a hand to stop me again. "The spot is still yours at Harvard. It is being held just for you. What do I need to do to get you to agree to go? That is all I want to know. I will do whatever it is so we can have this situation wrapped up before I take office."

"I'm not going to law school, Father. Not now, not ever."

"Reagan, be reasonable—"

"No, you're not listening to me. You've *never* listened." I stood up and started pacing the room, my eyes glued to my father's deep blue ones. "Look, as twisted as it is, I appreciate the offer. But I'm NOT interested. I don't want to be a lawyer. I've been telling you that for years. And for *years* you've refused to hear me. Maybe you didn't believe me, or maybe you just didn't care." I pointed at him. "I'd put money on the latter. Because everything you do, every plan you make, is only for your benefit. You have never once treated my life like it belongs to me." I stopped walking and stared at him. "But it is *mine*. JUST mine."

"But you're wasting your—"

"I'm not wasting a fucking thing!"

"Reagan, I will not sit here and listen to you talk to your father like that."

I waved toward the door. "You're welcome to go stand outside and wait until I'm done,

Mother."

She clutched her pearls, glanced at the door, but didn't make a move to leave.

"I'm finally doing something I love," I said to my father. "And I'd think you, of all people, should understand that. Yeah, it's not something *you* love—I get that. I also know that you're never going to understand why I love it. That's fine. You don't have to. But it would be nice if you simply acknowledged my passion and supported me for once in your life. I love art. I live and breathe art. I have an incredible eye for talent, and I've been gathering contacts in the art world to be able to sell people's art. I'm working toward owning my own gallery someday."

My parents sat perfectly still, sporting matching shocked expressions. My hands were shaking, my heart pounding. I'd never been so open with them about my passion. I nervously twirled the ring Dare had given me, suddenly realizing that they didn't know about that either.

I held up my left hand. "And I'm going to marry Dare."

I shouldn't have been surprised by their horrified gasps, but I was startled. And hurt. Why couldn't they see him the way I saw him?

My mother sprung to her feet, bright red lips

thinned into a hard line, polished fingers flexing for a martini glass.

"Sorry, Mother. I don't have any Xanax or gin to offer you to help soften the blow."

"That's enough, Reagan." My father stood and grasped her hand in his. "I am sure you can imagine how this hurts us."

"How *what* hurts you?"

"The fact that our daughter is marrying so far beneath her." There were tears in my mother's eyes. Actual. Fucking. Tears.

"I don't know how we can spin this," my father said, turning to look at my mother.

"Spin this? Are you fucking kidding me?" I sputtered for a moment, words failing me as outrage flooded my body. "I LOVE him. He is the love of my life. My fucking soul mate. Shouldn't you want your daughter to marry the right *guy*, not just someone who comes from the right *family*? Are you that self-absorbed and selfish? Isn't my happiness important to you AT ALL?"

"Of course it is." My mother snapped, her words clipped and sharp. "Your happiness has always been important. We have done everything in our power to make you happy and you have never appreciated a single thing we did. We sent you to the right school, introduced you into the right circles, encouraged you to socialize with the right friends. We have paid for everything you ever needed and then some. And all you have ever done is complain. And I, for one, am tired of it, Reagan. Nothing we do is good enough for you. It never has been and it never will be."

"You didn't do any of that for me," I said. "You did it for *you*. Because *you* want me to have the right friends, to marry into the right family, to have the right career…according to what *you* think is right. Not according to how I feel. And those 'right' friends you introduced me to? One of them raped me. Which you covered up like it was some minor, bothersome blemish. And then when it was obvious I'd gotten—"

"ENOUGH." My father's voice boomed through the small room. I was breathing heavy, glaring at them both. "We are not here to rehash the past." I raised my eyebrows, and opened my mouth to speak, but he beat me to it. "What do you want from us, then, Reagan? If we've made your life so unhappy, what do you want from us now?"

Just like that, all the fight flew out of me. My shoulders drooped, and I sighed.

What did I want? Deep down really I just

wanted them to love me. That was all I'd ever
wanted from them. But that wasn't ever going to
happen, and they wouldn't understand what I
meant if I actually said those words anyway.

So I just said, "I want you to let me live my life.
Pretend that you approve of my choices, let me
make my own mistakes, and support my right to do
that. Let me be happy. If you refuse to do that, then
I want you to get out of my life. For good. Forever."

My mother sniffed. My father simply nodded.

"We will try to respect your wishes," he said
slowly.

"Fine. Then start by giving me space." I couldn't
let them into my life yet. I'd been burned by them
one too many times. "I'll call when I'm ready to see
you again." When and *if*, I couldn't help but think.

My father nodded toward the door. "Very well,
Reagan. As you wish."

I followed them to the door, watching my
mother wrinkle her nose again and wanting to
strangle her.

"How can you live in a place with no doorman
at the very least?" she said. "There is no security
here. Is this place safe?"

I'd been asking myself that same question ever
since I'd come home. Every sound set me on
edge—especially when Dare was out. I didn't

open the door if I didn't recognize the person knocking. I'd just clutch the baseball bat I kept nearby, ready to strike, my heart racing, my palms sweating, until the person went away.

Only then could I breathe again.

I felt the panic creep up at my mother's words as she studied the door. "Are those locks strong enough?" she said. "How do you keep the riffraff out?"

The door opened then, startling all three of us. My eyes darted for the bat—out of reach. But it was Dare. His eyes grazed over my parents, and landed on me, warm and worried. He knew how I was these days. I gave him a weak smile.

"Oh." My mother gave him a slow, scrutinizing onceover as she walked by, her mouth twisted in distaste, then paused in the doorway to turn and say, "I see you don't."

eleven
Reagan

By the beginning of December, we'd finished packing up Rex's stuff, donating what we could, saving what we couldn't part with, and storing everything Dare wasn't sure what to do with. There were many of Rex's personal belongings that he refused to sell, but he also couldn't bear to bring them to our place. At least not yet.

And I totally understood that.

Everything was infused with Rex, and every time we went to his house or touched his things it hit us again. I kept expecting to find him behind his easel, at the stove in the kitchen, or just around the corner. I swore I could still hear his voice resonating in the now-empty rooms.

We could feel the echo of his life—of *him*—and with it came the fresh pain of his loss.

I knew what I felt was a fraction of what Dare

was going through—I could see the darkness creep up in his eyes every so often, and I wished there was some way for me to take away his pain.

But there wasn't. There never would be.

So I did everything I could to fill our lives with happiness.

Not long after my parents' visit, I went back to the women's shelter on 132nd Street where I'd volunteered before. In previous years, Sabine had sponsored an art show right before the holidays for the kids to be able to show their work, maybe even make a sale or two. Since Sabine was in Europe, I'd called up the volunteer coordinator and offered to help get the students get ready and run the entire show.

For the past two weeks, I'd spent three afternoons a week supervising the art class, bringing in whatever supplies the kids needed, and helping guide the young artists.

It felt so good to be useful again.

It also felt great to not be jumping back into the world with both feet yet. Baby steps, they'd called them in rehab. One thing at a time, one day at a time. I simply wasn't ready for full-time again. And forcing myself to get out of the apartment a few times a week was hard enough. But I did it.

Those kids needed me.

Almost as much as I needed them.

Most of the time I stayed in, though, seeking shelter in my safe, little world with Dare. He tried to get me to go out more often—to dinner, an opening, a new gallery—but I felt too exposed. Too unanchored.

It didn't make sense. I knew that. I didn't need a therapist to point out that I'd been in the safety of Rex's house when hell had unleashed its mangiest hound. And even though I kept reminding myself that Daren was dead—that he couldn't ever come after Dare or me again—it still took everything I had to walk out the door.

My heart gave a little jump every time the door opened.

Like right now.

"Hey," I said, pressing my hand to my chest, wondering when my heart would stop doing that. If ever. I wasn't sure I could take a lifetime of these moments of fear and uncertainty.

Dare took one look at me, closed the door, crossed the room, and wrapped me in his arms.

"You're safe, baby," he said, kissing the top of my head.

"I know." I squeezed my eyes shut, pushing my face into his chest, breathing in his calmness. "And yet I don't."

He ran his hands up and down my arms. "Give it time." His chin rested on the top of my head and I could feel my heart return to its regular rhythm.

"So, how'd it go?"

"The insurance?" He shrugged. "It's not much."

"What? You lost twenty-three paintings in the explosion. How can it *not* be much?"

His head was shaking before I even finished. "Because I'm a nobody," he said. "They don't agree with the value I placed on my art. They're giving me less than half." His hands came down on my shoulders as I opened my mouth in indignation. "It doesn't matter, Ree. They're gone—there's nothing I can do about that."

"But it's not fair! You're an amazing artist and those paintings are worth—"

"Nothing." He slid his hands down my arms, grasped my hands in his and raised them to his lips. "It's okay. At least I'm getting some money out of it. It'll keep us going while I build up my portfolio again."

"So, you're going to…"

"Start painting again?" He pressed his lips together and nodded. "He'd be so pissed if I didn't, you know?"

It had been eight weeks since Rex had died.

Eight weeks since Dare had set foot in his own studio, let alone touched a brush.

Art was his lifeblood—it flowed through his veins, beat in his heart. I couldn't imagine Dare without his art—it was such an integral part of him, he couldn't be whole without it. Actually he *hadn't* been. Not fully. Not since Rex.

But today was different. I could see it in his face. He was back.

"I *need* to paint," he said, and I threw my arms around his neck and kissed him, my heart filling at his words.

"What can I do to help?" I started for the kitchen. "You need coffee? I'll put some water on. I'll be—"

"What I really need right now is a model." He trapped my wrist to stop me from moving. Lifting one eyebrow at me, he grinned. "How about it, Muse?"

I shook my head. "Dare…I don't think…." There was a horrible red scar in the middle of my phoenix. I hated every time I saw it in the mirror—it was too much of a reminder. And so I always kept it covered up. What he was asking for was—

"Ree. All I want to do is paint. *Finally.* And all I want to paint is you." He pinned me with his gaze and closed the distance between us. "Only you." His fingers slid under my long-sleeve tee and pulled it over my head.

I grabbed the camisole I had on underneath and tugged it down, covering my scar.

"I would," I said as I took a few steps back and bumped against the wall, "but I've got to…"

"You've got to what?" His hands reached for the waistband of my jeans and he popped the button open. "Make coffee? I can do that myself. But I'm not thirsty for coffee right now." He knelt in front of me, his gaze locked on mine as he slowly slid the zipper down.

I swallowed hard as his fingers brushed against my panties, starting a fire in my core that was quickly spreading throughout my entire body. Ever so slowly, he slid my pants down, his hands setting my skin ablaze as they trailed down my legs.

A throbbing ache was growing between my thighs and I moaned as he slid one hand up to cup my calf and lifted my foot out of the pant leg, and then again on the other side. He leaned forward and kissed one inner thigh, up, up, up until he was almost at my center, then he kissed his way down the other.

Panting, aching, alive with his touch, his name

slid between my lips as my nails dug into his
shoulders. His hot breath skated over me while
his fingers curled around the top of my panties.

"Was there anything else that you needed to
do?" He bathed my core in warmth, his words
caressing the spot where I wanted him most.

"The shelter…I have to…"

"You will. Tomorrow. Today, you're home." He
started inching the lace down over my hips.
"Lucky for me." As the fabric slid down my
thighs and fell to the floor, he added, "Because
I'm in desperate need of a model. And only you
will do." Dark eyes holding me captive, he leaned
forward until he was a whisper away from my
ache. "Say you'll pose for me, Ree."

Oh, god. His breath against my swollen clit sent
shivers up my spine.

"I'll pose for you." My voice was breathless.
"I'll do anything."

"All I'm asking is for you to let me paint you."
His tongue flicked against me as he laughed. "But
I'll keep that in mind." Warmth spread from his
mouth to the rest of my body as my hips began to
rock. When he stopped licking me, I whimpered
in protest. "You're still wearing too many
clothes," he said. "I paint nudes, remember?"

His hands gripped the camisole I was wearing

and started lifting it as he rose to his feet, his hard body sliding up mine.

"Wait…" I clamped my arms down on my sides, and he paused, quirked an eyebrow in silent question. "The scar…" I shook my head, not meeting his eyes. "It's just…I'm…"

"You're beautiful," he said, dropping the shirt and cupping my face in his hands. "The scar doesn't change that. No amount of scarring would." He pressed a gentle kiss to my lips, making me melt into him again. He reached for the hem of my shirt. "Let me paint you. Let me show you how incredible you are."

Searching his eyes, I found only love and truth reflecting back at me. Well, love, truth, and *lust*. They burned equally bright.

"Okay." I nodded and he lifted the shirt over my head, threw it to the floor. His hands skimmed my sides, his fingers barely tickling the shiny red skin marring my beautiful tattoo.

"Does it still hurt?" he asked. I shook my head as he leaned down to press his lips against it, and the heat of his kiss shivered through me. His eyes met mine. "Once it's totally healed, I can cover it, fill in the tattoo, if you want."

"I do," I said. "I want my phoenix to be whole again. I want to be whole."

"You already are." Dare's lips grazed my hip, his tongue following the lines of the tattoo as they swooped and swerved up my ribs. Then his hands cupped my breasts as his lips found my nipple. My head fell back, and I arched into him. His thumb teased my other nipple as he sucked the sensitive flesh, spreading tingles all the way down to my center.

He lifted his head and I opened my eyes to find him gazing at me.

"I want to paint you just like this," he said, his fingers caressing my face. "Overflowing with love and radiating lust." He pulled me against him, the hardness in his jeans rubbing me just right. "You are my best work, Ree. You always have been and always will be."

He burned a path of kisses across my chest and down the center of my stomach before heading south as he knelt in front of me again.

His hands slid up my legs and grasped my hips. And then his warm, wet mouth took me in, covering my ache with kisses as he licked me over and over again. My thighs opened on instinct and my hips rocked with him. Moans floated past my lips as I wove my fingers into his dark waves.

And when his lips closed around my throbbing clit, I lost the ability to do anything but feel. Feel him everywhere. Tingling spread from my core up into my abdomen and chest, then all the way out to my fingers and toes. My whole body electrified under his touch as his tongue undulated against me, his lips sucking, sucking, sucking, the intensity building until I was calling out his name over and over again as the waves rocked through me.

As the spasms ebbed, I tightened my grip on his hair and pulled him up. When his lips were level with mine, I took them, bruising them with the fervor of my love.

His fire matched mine, kiss for kiss, flame for flame.

"How do you do that to me?" I whispered against his mouth. "How do you burn me up and rebuild me every single time?"

"You're my phoenix," he said, his lips smoldering my skin. "And I'm yours. Two parts. One whole. Never forget that."

twelve
Reagan

"Did you notice Denny's sniffly nose?" Maya came up behind me and pointed across the meeting room at the short, stocky construction worker with cropped black hair. He sniffed again, and wiped his nose on his sleeve. Gross.

I looked at her. "Maybe he has a cold?"

"Or maybe he's using again." She tapped her bare wrist. "It's that time of the year for him."

"Seriously?"

"Like clockwork. He hates the holidays—always slips up mid-December." She eyed him again, holding her coffee cup up under her nose and inhaling its bitter scent. "You can tell by his eyes—glassy, pupils so huge I can see them all the way across the room. Shit, I could probably walk right through them."

"Wow," I said, pouring hot water into the paper cup holding my tea bag. "You're good."

"Well, you know what they say—takes one to know one. Plus, I've been coming to these meetings since I was fifteen. I've seen it all." She blew her hair out of her face. "And many times over."

Maya was a year or two older than me, had intelligent dark eyes and jet-black hair cut in a severe bob that barely skimmed her chin. She was dressed in all-black as usual—oversized sweater, turtleneck, and short, flirty skirt. Her black platforms had her towering over me.

I'd liked her the moment I met her. There was something undeniably real and fresh about her. She was honest in a way that only recovering addicts ever could be—real about herself, her fuckups, and not afraid to call bullshit on others.

Every week, I looked forward to seeing her.

I'd been coming to this particular meeting ever since I'd gotten out of the hospital. It wasn't far from my volunteer work, and it took place in the breathtaking Riverside church—right at the edge of Columbia's campus. There was something about being inside the structure and surrounding myself by its beauty that gave me strength. After all, art touched me on a cellular level. And this gorgeous building was one hell of a piece of art.

So I kept coming, once a week, on my way to

the shelter. Sometimes twice if I felt like I needed it. Getting through another seven days clean, being able to show my face here and say in all honesty that I'd made it another week without succumbing to temptation kept me going.

Seeing Maya each time made it even better.

We took our cups over to the circle of chairs and sat down, and I listened to her prattle on about the other regulars as they filed into the room.

I was at home. Maybe an AA group was a fucked up version of home by most people's standards, but I felt safe. I belonged.

And I was on my way to recovery.

One step at a time.

After the meeting, I parted ways with Maya, and headed out of the church, psyching myself up for the five-block walk to the shelter. It was either that or taking a cab, and today I just wanted to breathe in the cold air and stretch my legs. I missed walking around this city of mine. And bit-by-bit, I was getting more comfortable with it again.

"Reagan! Reagan, over here!"

"Miss McKinley!"

Voices called out to me—none that I recognized—and I was suddenly surrounded by reporters flashing cameras and shoving microphones in my face. My first thought was that something had happened to Dare. That somehow his father wasn't actually dead and something huge had gone down. After everything I'd been through and considering my father was the governor-elect, my name was still too ever-present on people's lips. Their memories may have been short, but not enough time had passed yet for them to forget me.

"Congratulations, Miss McKinley! You must be so thrilled about your plans."

My plans? The reporter, a tall brunette in a bright red coat, waved around a copy of The New York Times, folded open to the wedding announcement page.

No. Fucking. Way.

I held out my hand for the paper, my eyes furiously raking over the text. Holy shit. My parents had placed the announcement for my wedding with a picture of me—and ONLY me—above it. There was no mention of Dare or his family at all. There was one buried line about my fiancé being an artist, but most of it was about my family, my father, the incoming governor of New

York. And—

Oh my god, there was a wedding date.

Dare and I hadn't set a date yet, but one for next fall glared back. They'd even picked a fucking location. It was all there, printed in fresh black ink.

My parents were trying to plan my wedding without even talking to me about it.

No. Fucking. Way.

I brushed off the reporters, and started jogging up the street toward Harlem, my phone already pressed to my ear.

My mother picked up on the third ring.

"Reagan," she said, her voice as smooth as butter. If reporters hadn't already assaulted me, I'd be trying to figure out why she was using her schmoozing tone with me. But I knew. All too well.

"How dare you?!" My voice shook as I hissed into the phone.

"Ah, you've seen The Times, darling. It's a wonderful piece isn't it? Now, I know that's an old picture we used, but we didn't have any recent shots of you. I hope you don't mind."

"Mind? You don't want me to mind the *photo* you used? What about the fact that you placed the announcement without my knowledge or consent? What about the fucking wedding date you've arbitrarily set? Not to mention the venue!"

"The Hamptons' estate is the perfect wedding location. It was perfect for Quincy's ceremony, it will be perfect for yours, too."

"You're not listen—MOTHER. You're not planning my wedding. Dare and I haven't even picked a date and you can't just take over—"

"Honestly, Reagan, I do not understand what the problem is. You asked for our support and here we are supporting you the best we know how. We have accepted your *artist*—" She said the word like it was a synonym for *leper,* and I could hear her shudder over the phone. "—and his sordid past, with open arms. What exactly are we doing wrong *this* time? Please do enlighten me."

"You had no right—" I stopped abruptly on the street, eliciting a curse from the person walking behind me. I couldn't have this conversation with her over the phone—it wasn't getting me anywhere and we'd just end up going around in circles. "You know what?" I said as I turned and strode back downtown. "I'm coming over right now. You two have got to stop meddling—"

"Your father and I are not home at the moment."

I halted and nearly tripped some other guy

behind me.

God, what was with people walking so fucking close? It was making me twitchy. I moved off to the side, leaning my back against a building as I watched the people passing by, looking for any signs that they were more than just fellow pedestrians, but every one of them ignored me.

God bless New Yorkers.

"Well, where are you?"

"Antigua. A little pre-inauguration vacation. Your poor father is going to be swamped soon. This is our last chance to really relax what with the holidays coming up and him taking office right after." She sighed dramatically, like her life was really all that hard. I rolled my eyes. "We will be back next Friday. Why don't you come over? You can admonish us then."

Next Friday. The day before the kids' art show.

"Fine." It would give me time to try to come up with a way to keep them out of my private business. This wedding stuff was just the tip of the iceberg with them. "Friday night."

I pocketed my phone and headed toward the shelter, trying to clear my mind and forget about my parents. Because in the end, they didn't matter. They could place all the announcements they wanted, but it didn't mean I had to go along with any of their wishes.

Not anymore.

I was living my own life now. And they were going to learn what that meant the hard way.

thirteen
Dare

"Did you see today's Times?" Ree threw down her bag, marched into the kitchen, and slapped the paper down on the counter right next to where I was chopping vegetables. "It's ENLIGHTENING."

"Really." I put the knife down on the cutting board and wiped my hands on the dishtowel. "How so?"

"Look at this crap!" She poked the facing page, and I leaned over it to skim the text beneath her picture. "Apparently, we're getting married next fall in the Hamptons. Congratu-*fucking*-lations to us!"

I glanced up and could practically see the steam coming out of her ears. "Wow. Sounds very blue blood," I said with a laugh. "Do you think we'll be invited?"

"Dare!" She smacked my arm. "My fucking parents—"

"Don't matter." My hands settled over her shoulders and I pulled her into me. Her arms snaked around my waist and she relaxed against me. "We'll get married our way," I said as I breathed her in. "Who cares what kind of bullshit they print in the paper. This is you and me, Ree. We are in control." She leaned back and looked up at me, her blue eyes shining. "We can get married whenever and wherever you want. Hell, we could even elope."

Her mouth quirked up. "Seriously? You'd do that?"

"Sure, baby. Anything you want." I leaned down to taste her soft lips, and she opened into my kiss with a sweet moan. Her hands fisted my t-shirt as she pulled me against her. I deepened the kiss, teasing her with my tongue, exploring her lips, then her jaw, slowly headed for her neck.

I brushed her hair out of the way and laughed. "You have paint on the side of your neck." I bit the tender flesh on her collarbone, then reached for a damp cloth. "How are the kids doing? All ready for their show?"

Her gaze suddenly lit up. "Oh my god, Dare. They are so amazing. Taye has this incredible pencil drawing he's been working on—it's this huge, detailed battle scene and I'm just so freaking proud of him. I can't wait to get it framed for the show. He's going to go nuts when he sees it hanging up on the wall." I tilted her head to the side and started to wipe the paint off as she continued to talk. "And Serena's little clay animals will be ready to be fired by the end of the week. She's going to glaze them at the pottery studio with me on Friday, then Janelle will fire them over the weekend. I'll pick them up on my way to the shelter on Monday afternoon." She clapped her hands together and kissed me again. "I can't wait for you to see the art these kids have created, Dare! They're real mini-artists. Every single one of them!"

Her excitement about this show and working with the children at the community center was one of the main reasons I'd said no to Amelie's offer this afternoon, and why I wasn't even going to mention it to Ree. She'd either have to drop everything so we could go to Paris or we'd have to be apart again for a few weeks.

And I was done with being apart.

Though the offer had been excruciatingly tempting. Amelie Marseille was the head of the renowned Paris Atelier d'Art, and was starting a new program of up-and-coming young artists. She'd gone to my show in Paris, bought a painting, then had gotten in touch with Rex when she couldn't reach me.

Apparently, she went way back with Rex as well.

After I started painting again, Rex sent her photos of my new stuff without telling me. She was interested in buying more paintings for her own collection, but also wanted me on her staff. After his death, she'd waited to contact me for as long as she could, but she needed me there right away. I'd be teaching classes, working on my own stuff, and showing my work to a much larger audience. It was the opportunity of a lifetime.

But I had to turn her down.

Ree wasn't ready to leave the country—she had a hard enough time leaving the apartment. And her work at the shelter was breathing new life into her. I couldn't ask her to give it up. Not this time. I couldn't risk losing her again. Everything was finally working out for us and there was no way in hell I was going to do anything to fuck it up.

Ree was much more important than my career. This might've been a great job, but she was my life. My heart. My soul.

I wiped the last of the paint off her neck, tossed the cloth onto the counter, and listened as she talked about her art class. She glowed when she spoke about the kids. I loved that.

The most beautiful thing about Ree was that she loved with her whole heart. And she opened it more easily now.

Which was so fucking sexy.

"Feeling better?" My eyes followed Ree as she crossed the room, naked, her long wet hair sending little droplets of water racing down her skin. My hands ached to feel her, my tongue longed to catch those drips and erase their paths, but from where I sat on the bed I couldn't deny I had the best vantage point to appreciate her in all her natural glory.

Damn. She was the sexiest woman I'd ever known, and she was all mine. Yeah, I was the luckiest fucking guy in the world.

She gave a little shrug and shot me a smile as she pulled one of my old t-shirts over her head.

"Don't worry about your parents," I said as she crawled into bed and curled against me. "We can handle them. Just focus on the good stuff—like the art show."

My hands slid under her shirt, exploring her bare skin, feeling her respond to my touch. She moaned as I cupped her breasts in both hands, gently rolling her nipples in between my fingers until they peaked. She arched her back and opened her legs for me.

And I was gone.

I slid my hand down her warm, soft stomach and paused there, imagining the future.

"I can't wait until you're doing art with our kids," I whispered into her ear. "You're going to be so fucking sexy when you're pregnant. I'm going to paint the shit out of you the whole nine months."

"Really?" She leaned up on her side, her face filled with wonder. "Even with a huge belly?"

"Especially then." I cupped her stomach, slid down and kissed it all around. "Because inside will be our own little work of art."

She pulled me up to kiss her and the feel of her tongue tangling with mine made my heart race.

"Let's do it now," she said. "Get married. Start our life together."

There was nothing I wanted more, but I also knew my family would kill me if they didn't get to be a part of it. And, truth be told, I wanted them there.

"How about over Dax's winter break? The first week of January. I'll fly him, Dalia, and my mom to New York. Dash'll be off, too. We'll go to City Hall. For New Year's. Maybe some of your family—"

"No." She shook her head. "Your family is my family. They've welcomed me into their hearts since day one. I only want them." She got an adorable evil grin on her face as she said, "My parents can just read about it in the paper."

fourteen
Reagan

"So," Dare said as he focused on the canvas, his brush making little flicking strokes, "we're on."

"We're on?"

"For New Year's Eve. Eleven a.m. Everyone will be here."

I lifted my head off the futon mattress, pressed a hand to my bare chest to calm my skipping heart.

"Really? Just like that?"

"What," he said, "like it's hard to set up a wedding? I made a couple of calls, arranged a few flights, and we're good to go." He grinned at me, then turned back to his canvas. "Now lie back down. You've messed up the pose."

"If I could marry you right now," I said as I lay down and smiled up at the ceiling, "I totally would."

"If you married me right now you'd be naked at

our wedding." He lifted a wicked eyebrow at me. "Which, come to think of it, could be a whole lotta fun. Instead of 'you may kiss the bride,' the officiant could say 'you may fu—'"

"*Dare!*" Even though I tried to sound indignant, I couldn't stop the laughter from bubbling out of me.

This was happiness. This right here with Dare. I wanted this to be our happily ever after right now.

The fact that we were doing this wedding on our own made me deliriously happy. That my meddling parents would be thwarted, even more so. I felt positively giddy about the whole thing.

"Do you mind much?" Dare said, breaking into my thoughts. A serious look had settled on his face, his eyebrows lifted and were almost touching in the middle of his forehead.

I had no idea what he was talking about.

"Doing it so small." He dipped his brush in more paint and dabbed it on. "I'm sure it's not how you imagined your wedding day."

I shook my head. "No, I don't mind. Small is perfect." It was exactly what I wanted, and exactly what my parents would hate the most. Which really didn't figure into my decision. Much. "Though I…" My voice trailed off as a picture flashed through my mind, but I shook off the image because it truly didn't matter.

"You what?" Dare had stopped painting and was looking intently at me. "What were you going to say?"

"Nothing. It's…nothing. *Really*." I didn't want to spoil any of his plans, didn't want him to think that I wasn't getting what I wanted, because the only thing I really wanted was Dare. And he was giving me exactly that.

"Ree," he said, his voice low, "tell me."

I sighed because there was no getting out of this. If I didn't tell him now, he'd just keep pressing me until I did. "I once saw this painting of a bride and groom in an outdoor, countryside ceremony. It took place at night, under the moon and the stars, lit with thousands of candles, their happy faces glowing in the warm light. Ever since then, I'd always envisioned my wedding exactly like that. But it's not important to me," I assured him quickly. "Marrying you is what's important. It's the only thing that truly matters."

"Aw, Ree. I'm sorry. I never even asked when I set it all up. I just—"

"No, it's fine." I sat up again. "It's perfect, really. I just want to marry *you*. I really don't care where or when, other than that it's soon."

He eyed me for a moment. "You sure?"

"Positive."

He nodded and turned back to his painting again, touching the canvas lightly with his brush. He'd been working steadily over the past few weeks, and it filled me up to see him at his easel again. He was content, and it showed in everything he did. Happiness colored his world again. And by default, it colored mine, too.

Every day he was in his studio. Most of the time I was here with him, except for the afternoons when I went to meetings and the shelter. I'd spent more time naked these past days than I had since we'd found each other again in Paris.

And, as I eyed him sitting over on his stool fully clothed, something occurred to me.

"I don't understand why I'm the only one who has to be naked here."

He didn't even look up from his work. "Because you're the model. And I paint *nudes*."

"Yes," I said, "but I would enjoy the view so much better if you were also *painting* in the nude."

The corners of his mouth lifted, but he shook his head. "I don't think that's a good idea."

"Oh, come on. It's not like you need to wear clothes to work." I bit my lip to stop myself from grinning as I said, "In fact, I dare you to take them off."

He turned toward me, his eyes narrowing, and carefully lay down his brush and palette. Then slowly he reached for the hem of his long-sleeve dark green shirt, and lifted it over his head. Without taking his gaze from mine, he tossed it to the floor, pulled the buttons free at his fly, and slid his jeans off.

Dare au naturel. Be still my fucking heart.

"Better?" he said, still staring at me.

I nodded, a wide smile on my face. "Hell, yeah. MUCH better."

"Can I get back to work now?"

"Absolutely."

Wearing nothing but his heart-stopping grin, he picked up his brushes again.

And I let my eyes feast on him.

His smooth skin rippled over his muscles, looking like waves on a sand dune. My gaze trailed from his fingertips up his strong arms to his shoulders, where muscle met more muscle. It then traveled south, along his carved sides, to the swell of his butt, and down his lean and muscular legs.

He was perfection. I was being painted by a human work of art.

"We should do this more often," I said, and his eyes flicked to my face as I licked my lips. A groan escaped his throat, and my gaze settled on the very obvious growing sign of his desire. "I have a whole new appreciation for art right now." Watching his erection grow, I spread my legs, reached down and slid my fingers along my folds. I was so wet, so turned on.

Dare refused to look away from me, his dark eyes growing even darker when he saw my fingers working. This time, his groan morphed into a ravenous growl.

Spurred on, I dipped my fingers into my opening, then slid them up to circle my clit, spreading my excitement over myself.

"Ree…" My name was a plea on his lips, and I could see how painfully hard he was now, as his eyes stayed glued to my every movement.

I moaned his name, aching for his touch, wishing as I thrust my fingers inside myself that it was his long, hard length there instead. But he wasn't moving. He just kept watching, entranced.

I needed him, and I needed him now.

So I rolled over onto my stomach, lifted up on all fours, spread my legs and arched my back, my throbbing core an offering.

"Take me," I said, looking over my shoulder at him. "Just like this."

"Fuck, Ree." His stool crashed to the ground

with a *bang*, sending my heart into overdrive as his quick, long strides brought him to me. "You're the best kind of muse I could ever ask for." The mattress dipped as he lowered himself behind me, his fingers slowly tracing my spine, savoring my skin as if it was a canvas. "My very own piece of artwork." With those words, his hands gripped my hips and, without hesitation, he thrust inside of me.

I cried out in ecstasy as he filled me completely. His palms slid up my back, then around to cup my breasts as he started to move. Skilled fingers teased my nipples into tight, hard buds, shooting thrills through my body, building up pressure within my core as he pumped in and out, in and out, increasing his pace with each thrust of his hips.

He rocked me hard, over and over again, and I called out his name, love filling my voice each time he plunged inside me. We moved in sync, connecting as one, our souls interlaced, heartbeats perfectly matched, bodies wholly entwined in this joint moment of ecstasy.

"Come with me, baby." His hands left my breasts and traveled down to my ache, where his fingers circled my swollen clit as he thrust into me faster and harder. I exploded into a thousand pieces just as he found his release.

As our spasms passed, we collapsed onto the mattress, and Dare pulled me against him, softly sucking on the tender skin at the back of my neck.

"This," he said, trailing kisses over to my shoulder, "is why it's a very, very bad idea for me to paint naked. I can't resist you, Ree. I need clothes to work—or else I'll never finish another piece. Though I guess that's the price to pay for finishing *off* other masterpieces."

"You won't hear this masterpiece complaining about that." I laughed, and he rolled me over then he kissed me breathless. "This is probably also why I shouldn't be naked at our wedding," I said as I ran my fingers through his dark waves. "We'd never make it to the vows."

"Then New Year's Eve it is," Dare said. "I'll be the one in clothes."

"So will I."

"And I will be the one to remove them afterwards," he added with a naughty wink.

"And forever after that," I said, and he nodded.

"Forever after, and then some."

fifteen
Reagan

"What do you guys think?" I took a step back and surveyed the studio. "Are we ready or what?"

Fourteen screaming kids tackle-hugged me, bringing me crashing down to the floor.

"Okay, okay!" I laughed, extending my arms out in an attempt to hug them all back. "I think that means we're a go for the show tomorrow afternoon. If you haven't invited all your friends and family members yet, make sure you give them a call tonight. But, for now, it's time to close the art studio." I struggled to my feet, little Jasmine still clinging to my neck. "Jazzy, I'll be back tomorrow. I promise," I said as I squatted down in front of her. "Your mom is going to be so proud of your paintings. You've worked so hard on them, and it shows."

The kids filed out, smiling and waving, as they all called out their goodbyes. I took one last look around the room and grinned. They'd done such amazing work, accomplished so much over the past few weeks. The room looked incredible. All of the art was exhibited professionally—countless colorful pieces lined the edges of the room. We'd spent the afternoon transforming the plain common room into a gallery, clearing out chairs and tables, hanging framed drawings and paintings on the wall, arranging sculptures to best show off their beauty, and then adding labels to identify the artists.

I was so freaking proud of these kids and what they'd accomplished, my heart was bursting with happiness. All I wanted to do was run home and tell Dare all about it. Or better yet, sneak him in here so I could show it to him right away.

But he was working on his latest painting, and I didn't want to disturb his peace when he was in the zone. Plus, he would be coming to the show tomorrow night.

And, unfortunately for me, I had somewhere to be. My parents were in need of yet another boundaries talk. Just the thought of having to spend the next hour with them set me off. I had no doubt they'd purposefully planned to be out of town when the wedding announcement ran in hopes that I'd have cooled down by the time they got back. Hell, deep down in her deranged mind, my mother had probably assumed I would "come my senses" and let them hijack my wedding.

Too bad for her.

Dare had offered to come with me and stand by my side as I reamed them out, but his presence wasn't necessary. This was my fight, and I was stronger now than I had been the last time I'd seen them. Plus, I was already in Manhattan, and he really needed to paint. He'd been working so hard, finding new models, trying to build up his portfolio again, and I wasn't going to let anything get in his way.

Honestly, I loved what he was doing. His new style was looser and wilder than before—harder lines, softer shadows, more vibrant colors. Something about his new technique—though I couldn't quite pinpoint *what*—made it appear as if his subjects were actually living and breathing on the canvas.

Yes. That was exactly it. His paintings were full of life, brimming with magic. More so than they'd ever been before. They had hope. You could almost hear the thoughts of each model.

The art was breathtakingly fresh and I had no doubt that he was on the verge of hitting it big. He just needed the right venue, the right opportunity, the right gallery show. First, though, he needed the paintings.

So while he worked, I grabbed a cab and headed for the hell that was New York's Upper East Side.

I had a whole speech planned out by the time I was in the elevator. And when the doors opened, I stalked out with my chin held high, my movement fueled by anger and determination.

But the sight in front of me stopped me in my tracks.

The entire penthouse was lit up with twinkling, white lights. Soft classical music filtered out into the hallway, accompanied by laughter and the clinking of glasses. People dressed in their fanciest holiday outfits roamed in and out of the entryway, and I could spot the edge of a huge Christmas tree towering over everyone in the ballroom.

The scene hit me square in the face, but it took a moment for it all to sink in.

My parents' annual holiday party.

And, fucking hell, they'd tricked me into showing up.

At least I took a little pleasure in the fact that I stood there in the midst of all those designer dresses and suits in paint-splattered, dust-covered jeans and a no-name, red cowl-necked sweater. I started to smile, imagining the distress it would cause my mother.

"Jesus, Reagan." Quinn's razor-sharp whisper caught me by surprise. "You look like a homeless person. Have you completely lost the ability to dress yourself? Don't tell me you actually wore this out in public?"

A biting retort tickled the tip of my tongue as I turned to face her, but I swallowed it when I saw what she had in her arms. Or, rather, *who*.

She beamed smugly at me. "This is Harrison. His pediatrician has cleared us to take him out in public as long as we don't let anyone else hold him."

Bright blue eyes stared at me as the little baby stuffed a chubby hand into his mouth and started sucking on it. His gaze widened for a moment as he chewed on his fingers, then he withdrew his hand and shot me a great big smile. And it was like the skies suddenly opened up in the middle of a rainstorm and the sun shone on me.

I reached out to him, but Quinn took a quick step back. "Don't touch him. You might have germs."

"Oh, relax." I offered him my finger and his sweet little hand closed around it. I stared at him transfixed for a moment, then looked up at my sister. "Did you say Harrison? Seriously? You actually named your kid Harry Truman?" I laughed. "Good god, Quinn."

"Harrison Nathaniel McKinley Truman, actually." Quinn sniffed, shifting the knit hat covering his head. "It's a perfectly respectable name. Pierce likes it. He got this huge smile when I told him."

"That's because he was laughing at you." Our brother got a lot of enjoyment at Quinn's expense. She just rarely realized it. I leaned toward Harry, and he reached for my face, his warm palm grazing my cheek. "Sorry buddy, but your mom's nuts."

"I am NOT."

"Reagan, you are finally he—" The words stuck in my mother's throat as her eyes took in the entirety of my outfit. She quickly scanned the room, an anxious look crossing her unnaturally young-looking face. Then she grabbed hold of my elbow and started pulling me toward the back of the apartment, hissing through her faux smile. "What is the matter with you? How could you show up here dressed like this? Do you want to embarrass us? Your father is the governor-elect, for goodness' sake!"

"Why, Mother, it's my holiday finest." I

smirked. "And if anyone should be embarrassed, it's you. You lied to me. Not to mention, you're a few too many martinis overdressed for our talk."

Ignoring me, she looked over her shoulder, back to where I'd been standing with Quinn. "You didn't bring your artist, did you?" She whispered the question like Dare was a dirty little secret, and I could feel my temper start to flare. "He would not fit in here at all."

"Neither do I." I ripped my elbow from her grasp, my mouth gaping as I realized what she'd done.

"Reagan, behave yourself—"

"You did this on purpose, didn't you? You didn't want Dare here, so you tricked me into coming tonight under the pretense that we'd be discussing your attempted wedding coup, but really you just wanted me to make an appearance at your fucking Christmas party. Another fucking photo op."

"You watch your language, Reagan Allison McKinley. You are amongst New York's elite, and you will act accordingly."

"What, Mother? You don't want me embarrassing you? You mean like you're embarrassing me with the man I love? That you would stoop to such a level..." I shook my head, tears stinging my eyes, my fucking heart breaking again. Why did I even bother when it came to my parents—the two strangers who'd given me life in the literal sense, but kept trying to take it away from me in every way possible? Why did I care what they thought or whether or not they welcomed Dare? I needed to walk away. It was time to snap the olive branch in half and get the fuck out. "You know what? If Dare isn't welcome here, then I'm not either." I glanced over her shoulder and nearly lost my shit. Every cell in my body wanted to freaking roar. "What the fuck is *he* doing here?"

My mother actually rolled her eyes. "Jackson Fitzgerald?" She didn't even have to turn around to know who I was talking about. Un-*fucking*-believable.

"He was supposed to be gone from your lives. Dad promised—oh my god." It felt like my life was crashing down on me again, and I was having a hard time getting a single breath in. "If he didn't think I was serious about the conditions I gave him, then he's going to be mighty surprised when I leak everything to the press. I'm done hiding. I'm done living with secrets."

"Oh, calm down, Reagan. No need to get hysterical." My mother huffed. "Jackson was not invited, he just showed up, and your father was not the least bit pleased. But what do you want us to do? He is the senator's son. Your father is the governor-elect. We cannot exactly throw him out without causing a scene. McKinleys do not make scenes. You know that."

"I don't give a shit about what McKinleys do or do not, Mother."

Jackson looked up to see me glaring at him and the smile he shot me had enough wattage to light up the city. But though his grin oozed charm and seemed to be dazzling the woman he was talking to, it didn't reach his eyes. They looked dangerously dark and cold. Shivers shuddered through me.

"You were able to manipulate me into coming, surely you and Dad could get a rapist to leave. I'm very aware of the range of your talents. The two of you together are sickeningly formidable." Jackson's eyes were on me again, and my skin began to crawl. I pointed down the hall, to my father's office. "I'm going in there while you get rid of Jackson and find Dad. I'll say what I came here to say to the two of you, then I'm leaving." She started to protest, her mouth open, her perfect blonde French-twist bobbing as she shook her head. "Unless, of course, you'd prefer to have our conversation out here in the middle of your party for everyone to hear." I shrugged. "It's up to you. I can talk as quietly or as loudly as you'd like."

My mother clamped her lips tight, reached up and touched her hand to her chest. Then she gave a curt nod. "Fine. We will join you in a moment, Reagan." She walked away, a fake smile plastered across her face.

Hands trembling, I pulled out my phone and called Dare. "You are not going to fucking believe what I just walked into." I filled him in on the clusterfuck that was this night.

He didn't even hesitate. "I'm on my way."

"Dare—"

"Ree, I'm walking out the door right now. I'm not leaving you alone with those people. And especially not with that fuckwad there."

"Thank you." I breathed, feeling my shoulders release just a bit.

I pocketed my phone again, turned, and came face-to-face with Jackson.

Fuck. Me.

"Reagan," he said, his voice cool and low. Hearing my name on his lips made me want to vomit. "I was hoping you'd show up." He blazed a smile at someone behind me, but I didn't dare take my eyes off of him. "We have some catching up to do."

"I have nothing to say to you, Jackson. My fiancé is on his way over, and I suggest you make yourself scarce before he gets here." I smiled coldly into his slimy face. "You remember him, don't you? From your encounter on the sidewalk?" His grin slipped a notch, and his eyes hardened. "I'm guessing he'll be even *less happy* to see you today. The only reason you're still breathing is because he hadn't known it was *you* that day. So you might want to clear out before he arrives."

Pushing past him, I hurried over to the elevator and pressed the button, fighting the urge to look over my shoulder, willing myself to just breathe. There was no way I was going to go wait in my father's office while my parents got their act together. Not when Jack was still here.

The doors opened, I slipped in, and hit the button for the ground floor. I got a glimpse of Pierce's worried face right before the doors slid shut.

The lobby was blessedly bare of people, save for the doorman who nodded at me as I paced in front of the windows to the street. The other elevator dinged, and my heart raced, fearing

Jackson had followed me down. But it was only some old rich guy I didn't recognize. I watched the doorman show him out, then hurry to the curb to hail him a cab.

I glanced at the time on my phone. It wouldn't take Dare long to get here, I knew. Not on his motorcycle, and especially not when he was pissed. So I only had to hang on for—

"You've ruined my life, you selfish bitch!"

Pain flared up my right arm as Jackson's fingers dug into it with the strength of a vice grip. I tried to pull away, but he only held on tighter. He spun me around to face him, his other hand clamping onto my left arm.

Gone was the charm and ease he'd been wearing upstairs. All that was left was craze.

"Do you have any idea how fucking hard I've worked on your father's campaign? How many hours I've put in? How much of my fucking life I've had to give up for that overblown douchebag?"

"No, and I couldn't care less." His hands squeezed tighter and I winced. "Jack, you're hurting me. Let go of my arms!"

"GOOD, you fucking cunt. Everything I've worked for is gone because of you. You've fucked with my career and you're going to pay for it."

"I'm going to *pay for it?* Are you fucking kidding me?" Pain was replaced with fury, and if he hadn't been holding my arms I would have punched him in the face. "I've been paying for it for seven fucking years already, you asshole. YOU ruined MY life. If things are going bad for you now, consider that payback for what you did." Seven years of anger and humiliation flowed out of me. "I'm tired of being ashamed of what YOU did. I'm tired of hiding." I held his gaze with mine. "And I'm not going to do it anymore. As soon as I leave this place, I'm going to report you to the police like I should have done all those years ago. You've gotten away with it for too long, but not anymore."

He suddenly released both of my arms, taking a step away from me as I stumbled back. Too late, I realized my mistake as his face contorted in maniacal rage.

I was already running when he shot after me.

sixteen
Dare

Her screams hit my ears as soon as I cut the engine on my bike. A moment later, I was flying through the doors, wondering why I couldn't hear her anymore.

And then I saw them.

Jackson was on top of Ree, his hands around her neck. Some guy in a maroon uniform was trying to pry him off.

I launched myself at Jackson, tucking my head and ramming it into his stomach. The momentum sent him tumbling backwards, throwing him off Ree. And then I was on him, fists flying, hardly feeling any impact at all as my punches connected with his jaw and cheekbones. So I hit him harder and harder, anger eclipsing all of my senses. Blood sprayed from his battered face, spattering my clothes.

And still I hit him. Over and over again.

Suddenly Ree was in front of me and someone was pulling me off the bastard. Jackson's hands covered his face as he rolled onto his side and just lay there in an unmoving, bloody heap.

The guy who had hold of me shoved me away from Jackson.

"Pierce!" Ree got in between us. "Leave him alone. Dare just saved my life." She lifted her chin and I could see the bright red marks around her throat where the prick's hands had been. My rage reignited, but she put a hand on my chest. "Don't. It's over. You'll kill him."

"With pleasure."

"No, Dare." She wrapped her arms around me, squeezed me tight. My own arms enveloped her instinctually. "If you did, you'd go to jail. I can't bear to be without you anymore."

"He's going to jail as it is," Ree's father said, his face livid. "He just attacked the son of a senator. Jackson will press charges, and this one will be sent where he belongs."

"*What?!*" Ree whipped around before I could even open my mouth to respond. "*Jackson* will press charges? Are you fucking kidding me?" She stormed over and stood her ground, practically nose to nose with him. "Jackson raped me when I was fifteen years old, and you swept it under the rug."

A crowd of people was growing in the lobby, all dressed like they'd come from the party. At Ree's statement there was a collective gasp, and her mother clutched her chest as if she was having a fucking coronary.

"He ruined my life and you LET him do it. You fucking LET him get away with it." Ree's voice was strong, echoing off the walls of the lobby, but filled with hurt. "You didn't even believe me when I told you what he'd done."

Her chest heaved and a sob broke through her words. I came up behind her and put my hands on her shoulders.

"Ree," I said. "You don't have to do this. Let's just leave. Fuck them."

She looked up at me, her eyes as dark as a stormy sea. "No." She shook her head. "There's something I've never told you because I was too ashamed. But I'm tired of being scared and ashamed. Tired of hiding. Tired of all the secrets that have plagued my life."

"Reagan Allison McKinley, if you think airing your dirty laundry is going to solve anything…" Her father's eyes narrowed and his gaze flicked anxiously around at all the people witnessing the scene.

"My dirty laundry?" She scoffed. "More like *yours*. What you did—"

"Why don't we just go back upstairs where we can talk about this in private," he said. It was part plea, part threat. "Reagan—"

"Oh, just shut the fuck up, Dad," Ree said, and her brother Pierce's eyes bugged out of his head as he stifled a laugh. It almost made me like the guy. Almost.

"Reagan! I will not have you talking to your father—"

"You're even worse than he is," Ree said, her voice going sad. "I trusted you, Mother. When it turned out I was pregnant and you were finally forced to believe me about Jack's attack, I fucking trusted you! But you drugged me…and when I woke up in the clinic bed to find out I'd had an abortion…"

Jesus. The words cut through my heart, and my soul bled for Ree. I wished more than anything that I could turn back time, save her, make sure she never felt this pain.

Tears were streaming down her face now, and it was killing me to watch her. But this was her fight. I understood that. I stayed with her, though, willing the strength of my love to keep her afloat.

"How could you?" she said. "How could you do

that to me? To that baby? How could you not even give me the choice? It was *my* body."

"Oh, for chrissakes, Reagan. You were fifteen years old. You weren't old enough to make such a decision. We simply did what was best for you at the time."

"A forced abortion was best for me?" She laughed, hollow and cold. "Do you want to know what it was like, Mother? It was like *getting raped a second time*. But, this time, it was my parents who did it."

"You have always gotten so hysterical about this. He was the governor's son, Reagan. What did you want us to do? Your father was getting into politics and we couldn't let something like this ruin his career. We had to look at the big picture."

"Is this true?" Quincy said, stepping forward, clinging tightly to the baby in her arms. She looked shell-shocked as she glanced back and forth between her parents. "You really did that to Reagan?" She was shaking her head like she couldn't believe her parents were capable of such a horrific thing.

Even after all I'd witnessed when it came to these people and the way they treated Ree, I was still surprised. If I could have gotten away with decking her father, I would have. But I'd already dug myself a big, fucking, U.S. senator-sized hole, and couldn't afford to make things worse by punching the governor of New York as well.

No matter how much he deserved it.

But this wasn't the fight I wanted to have now. Not when all I wanted to do was wrap Ree in my arms and take her far, far away from these monsters masquerading as her parents.

Pierce walked over to stand next to Ree and placed his arm over her shoulder. And Quincy came over to her other side.

Holy fucking shit.

Ree looked from Pierce to Quinn, wonder filling her eyes.

"I thought you'd finally decided to support me, but after tonight, after everything you've done…" She held out a finger to Quinn's kid and he grabbed hold of it. Then she looked at her parents again. "I can't believe in you—either one of you—and I certainly can't trust you."

"Oh, honestly, Reagan! The dramatics are at an all-time high with you. Perhaps you should be an actress rather than an art dealer." Her father threw up his hands, trying to laugh off the situation, but no one in the crowd laughed with him.

Ree's head snapped up and her eyes turned to steel. "Fuck. You. I'm done with you. Forever. I'll never, ever let you come near my future children. Not after everything you've done. And the saddest, most disturbing part of this all is the fact that you clearly don't think you were ever in the wrong."

"You will stop this now, Reagan," her mother said, her words flung at Ree like slaps. "This is all in the past, and the only one holding onto it is *you*—clinging to it in a last desperate attempt for attention." Her voice echoed around the marble-covered room. "And your threat is laughably empty, my darling. Because it's not like you can actually have children, anyway."

Her mother's cold laugh was the only sound in the deafening silence.

seventeen
Reagan

Time stopped, my mother's words rang in my mind as the echo of her laugh died away.

There was only shocked silence in the aftermath. It vibrated in my ears, seeped into my body, tunneled deep into my heart.

The hair stood up on my arms as her words hit me.

"What did you just say?" My breaths were coming faster and faster, as I desperately tried not to hyperventilate. "What do you mean…I *can't* have children?"

My mother's eyes widened as if she hadn't realized what she'd just let slip. She took hold of her pearls, clutching onto them for dear life. As if that was fucking going to save her now.

In a low voice she said, "Perhaps it would be best if we all went upstairs and discussed this matter in the privacy of our home."

"Why? Are you embarrassed, Mother? You just announced to half your guests that I can't have children and YOU'RE suddenly embarrassed?" I shook my head, begging it to stop spinning, pleading with my heart to slow down and my voice to quit shaking. "No, we'll finish this discussion here because I will not be setting foot in your house ever again." I took a deep breath. "Why, exactly, can I not have children?"

"There was an infection after the...*procedure*...and the doctor told us it rendered you sterile." At least she had the sense to look slightly abashed as she spoke, even if it was too little, too late.

Waking up in that hospital bed, my mother by my side, I remembered being confused. I'd asked her groggily if my appendix had burst.

She'd laughed in response. "Oh, don't be so dramatic, Reagan. It was nothing like that. We simply took care of that little problem of yours."

I hadn't understood what she meant, fevers and pain driving me to the brink of madness. But she made it perfectly clear later on—I was stunned, and felt violated to the depth of my soul. And even though I'd been on heavy antibiotics for a month, it never occurred to me that something had gone wrong. I had thought it was just part of the pain that came with recovery.

That was when my love affair with pills had started. I'd craved the numbness like a fucking junky.

If I didn't have Dare grounding me with his hands on my shoulders right now, an unconscious reminder of all the reasons not to succumb, I'd be aching for a bottle of pills again. I couldn't even form words to respond to my mother's revelation.

Eyeing me, she added, "Which didn't seem like a big deal because you've never wanted children anyway."

My eyes blinked furiously as my mind fought to keep up with the implications of everything she was saying. My whole future suddenly felt like it was on shaky ground.

I wanted kids. Dare wanted kids. If I couldn't have kids…where did that leave us?

"It didn't seem like a *big deal?*" Quinn said next to me, her voice laced with disgust. "How could you keep this from Reagan? From all of us?" She looked like she was seeing our parents for the first time. That had to hurt after a lifetime of delusion.

It still hurt *me* even though I'd been seeing them clearly for years.

But this was a whole new level of clarity I was getting right now.

My father shrugged his shoulders. "We were doing what was best for Reagan."

Dare's hands slipped from my shoulders and in the back of my mind I felt their absence hit me in the gut. But I was far too focused on my parents to turn and look at him.

No, instead I lost it.

"That is bullshit!" I didn't care about the shocked expressions on their guests' faces or the fact that some of them even had their phones trained on me. Nothing mattered at this point. "You were doing what was best for YOU. What you've always done. And you trying to justify it now is absolutely ridiculous. And cowardly." I waved my arm around the room at all the people watching and listening. "I hope this fucking ruins you. Can you see the headlines now? 'Governor-Elect Forced Fifteen Year Old Daughter to have Abortion.' 'Former Mayor Drugs Daughter, Tricks her into Abortion after Letting Her Rapist Go Free.' I don't think there's any way you'll be able to spin THAT."

"We got a call about a disturbance here?" A bulky male police officer and his female counterpart strode between us.

The woman looked at my father, then down on the floor where Jack lay moaning. "Mayor

McKinley, what happened here? Who beat this man?"

My father's eyes were locked on mine when he lifted his finger and pointed at Dare. "He did it, officers."

I turned around and reached for him, but Dare was back by the door, already holding out his wrists for the cop to cuff him.

"NO!" Shaking my head, I started toward him, but the policeman stepped in to block my way.

"I'm sorry, miss, you cannot interfere with an arrest."

"He was protecting me!" I cried, not taking my eyes off Dare. But he was staring at the ground, refusing to meet my gaze. Oh, god. Why wasn't he looking at me? "I just need a moment with him." I looked up at the officer, pleading with my eyes.

He shook his head.

"You should be arresting THAT GUY—" I pointed at Jackson who was still on the floor, getting looked over by a paramedic. "—because he was trying to kill me. Dare saved my life! You can't arrest him. You can't take him away from me—"

"We'll be happy to take your statement at the station later tonight."

I opened my mouth again, but Pierce's arm closed around my shoulders. "Don't make it worse," he whispered in my ear. "Just cooperate and let them do their jobs, Reagan. We'll get this sorted out. I promise."

Dare still hadn't glanced my way. Not even as he was being led outside to a waiting police car.

"Pierce, you've got to help him. *Please.*" Panic rose within my chest, threatening to choke me. "He saved my life. But he has a record and Jack's dad is a senator...they're not going to listen to Dare. He's going to get totally screwed by the system. I can't—" My words cut off as my throat closed. I had to swallow and force the rest through. "I can't lose him. *Please.*"

If Dare even still wanted me. What if he'd changed his mind after hearing about the baby? What if that was why he wouldn't meet my eyes, just to let me know that he was okay, that *we* were okay. I'd kept my deepest, darkest secret from him. And he'd just found out I couldn't have kids, after we'd spent countless nights lying in bed and talking about the future. My heart was breaking at the thought, and his had to be, too. But just because I couldn't have kids didn't mean that he couldn't. He could find someone else...

Oh, god.

Why wouldn't he look at me?!

"Just tell the police what happened," Pierce said to me. "Dare will do the same. It'll be both of your words against Jack's. I'm sure he'll be released by tomorrow morning. Maybe even later tonight." He squeezed my shoulder. "Don't worry about it, Reagan. Justice will be served."

But when I glanced across the room at my father talking to some officers, I knew that justice couldn't ever be guaranteed when he was involved.

eighteen
Dare

Sitting in a cell, wondering whether the hell I was going to get out of here anytime soon was torture. I'd told the police what happened. Play-by-play. Several times. And they'd come back at me with charges that I'd attacked the senator's son unprovoked.

Fucking hell.

Just when our lives were coming together, I had to go and screw it all to hell. I couldn't believe I'd fucked up like this. Beating the shit out of Jackson had felt good. Too good. And that stupid mistake had landed me here. Possibly for a long time if the senator and mayor had their way.

As soon as the cops had shown up, I'd known it was over. That I was going to pay. I couldn't even look at Ree, couldn't stand to see the disappointment I knew had to be in her eyes. I'd fucked everything up—our past, our present, and definitely our future.

A door clanged open down the hall, then an expensive suit strode into sight and stopped in front of my cell. Great. Ree's fucking brother.

"Fuck off," I said before he could even open his mouth.

"And good evening to you, too," Pierce said. "It must've been your charm that first caught my little sister's eye."

"If you're here to finish off your father's dirty work, you don't need to talk to me. Go spin your story, tell your lies to the cops, but just leave me the fuck alone."

Pierce laughed. "Ah! You are like a breath of fresh air. No wonder Reagan loves you. Tell me, before we get down to business, do you happen to have a sister?"

I was off the bench, my arm through the bars, and had him by his tie before he could even blink.

He cocked an eyebrow at me. "All I have to do is call '*Officer!*' and you'll have even more problems on your plate. You sure you want that? I'm here to help you."

I released him, and wrapped my hands around the bars. "I don't need your kind of help."

Pierce shrugged. "Jack was released almost immediately, given that he's Senator Fitzgerald's son. I could have you out in an hour so you could go home to Reagan tonight."

"No, thanks," I said, shaking my head. "I'll do this on my own. I don't want to owe anything to anybody named McKinley."

Pierce looked at me for a moment, quirked his head, then said, "Don't you owe your life to Reagan?"

I sat back down on the bench. Hard. Yes, I did owe my life to her. And I didn't want her to see me like this. I'd told the police to not let her in if she came by—because I knew she would come, but I just couldn't bear for her to see me behind bars.

I was not my father's son. I didn't want to turn into the bastard, and I especially didn't want Ree to see me as him, as a monster, as some rageaholic. Not to mention, I refused to pull her into this mess. She didn't need her name getting dragged through the mud for a second time today. Besides, the truth was on my side in this case. The truth had to count for something.

Though, in my experience with the bluebloods of Reagan's world, truth was not a fixed black or white thing. It was malleable, shaped to benefit the rich and powerful.

And I was neither.

God, I was fucked.

"Let me help you, Dare. For Reagan," Pierce said. "Let me see what I can do."

"And what am I going to owe you? I've seen how your world works. Nothing is ever easy. Nothing comes free."

"Just my sister's happiness." Pierce started walking back down the hall toward the front desk. "After everything she's been through, she deserves that in spades."

Ree's happiness.

That was all I wanted, too.

nineteen
Reagan

He didn't come home.

I waited all night, pacing in front of the door, willing him to walk through it, flinching at every little noise. Being alone, I was reliving everything that had happened at Rex's and all that had followed. People's voices out on the street as they walked by sent my heart hammering.

What if Daren sent his men? What if Jackson was out for payback? What if Dare wasn't coming back?

If I'd been smart, I would have taken Pierce up on his offer and crashed with him last night. But I was so sure Dare would be released, and I didn't know what was going on with him, where we stood, since he'd been acting so strange once the police arrived. The last thing I wanted was to have him come home to an empty house. I didn't want him to doubt me for a moment.

But he didn't come home.

Unable to wait another second, I caught a cab to the precinct. I had no idea what their hours were, and I didn't really care. Officers had to be on duty 24/7, so they had to be open even at five in the morning.

And they couldn't keep Dare locked up for much longer. Could they?

I'd given my statement last night. I was sure the doorman must have given his. He'd seen Jackson attack me and had been the one who'd gotten my parents and called the cops in the first place. There was no way they could make any charges stick no matter who the hell Jack's father happened to be.

Though, with my father having his hands in this mess, nothing was certain. He'd probably dug out all the stuff he had on Dare and offered it to the cops. But none of that had any bearing on the truth of what happened, and I was going to explain that to whoever would listen. I'd scream it from the roof of the police station if I had to.

After the cab dropped me off, I hurried into the building.

A young cop with kind brown eyes looked up at me from the front desk. "Can I help you, miss?"

God, I hoped so.

"I'm here to see Dare Wilde."

"Name?" He typed something into his computer and watched the screen.

"Reagan McKinley."

His eyes flicked to my face, surprise filling his features. Then he glanced at his screen again, and started to slowly shake his head. "I'm sorry, Miss McKinley. He's...not able to have any visitors right now."

I clenched my fists, fighting the urge to start screaming that they had to let me in, that I needed to see him. Instead, I took a deep breath and said, "When can I come back to see him?"

He looked at me again, his eyebrows lifting to meet in the middle. "I'm sorry. We've been given instructions that he is not to see anyone but his lawyer."

Translation: *He doesn't want to see you, Reagan.*

The air flew out of my lungs like I'd been punched in the gut.

So that was it. I was damaged goods and he didn't want me anymore. That had been the reason he wouldn't look at me last night. Pain cracked my soul, working its way through me in jagged jolts with every beat of my breaking heart. I pressed a hand to my chest, unable to stop the tears. I stumbled back, and the officer came around the desk to lead me over to a bench.

"You okay?"

No. Not in the least. Everything was falling apart. How could this be happening?

"Miss?" The policeman handed me a cup of water and lowered himself down next to me. "For what it's worth, your parents should be put away for what they did to you. It's reprehensible."

"Huh?" I glanced up at him, certain that he couldn't be talking about what he was clearly talking about. How would he know? Behind him, several other cops were looking our way with sympathetic looks on their faces.

He must have noticed my confusion, because he pulled out his phone and typed something into it. "It's the biggest story of the day," he said, holding it out to me.

Shit. There it was. Right on The New York Times webpage. A picture of my father and one of me under the headline **Governor-Elect Has Explaining To Do—Buried 15 Year Old Daughter's Rape, Forced Abortion**. There was a detailed article about the entire sordid event that I was certain would be plastered all over newsstands today.

Well, I'd wanted to stop hiding—I guess sometimes you got exactly what you asked for.

I wasn't sure whether to laugh or cry.

Some tiny part of me was relieved, but mostly I just felt numb. All I wanted was peace. And Dare.

"Is he okay?" I said to the officer. "Dare? Is he…are you going to release him today?"

"He's fine, but I don't know any details regarding his case. I'm sorry."

"Isn't there anything you can do? Anything at all?" I was desperate. "Is there any way I can see him? Please?"

He shook his head. "I really can't help you. I truly am sorry, Miss McKinley."

Shit.

I drew in a slow, shaky breath, not wanting to face all the crap that was sure to come following the revelations of the article, and not sure where to go now. What to do.

I needed to know where I stood with Dare, but that wasn't going to happen until he was released. Which meant I needed to see Pierce and find a way to get him out as soon as possible.

But, first, there was something else that I could do. That I *needed* to do. Something that was seven years overdue.

I stood up, cleared my throat, and turned to the officer. "Actually, there *is* something you can help me with." My pulse raced as I spoke. "I want to file a report. Against Jackson Fitzgerald." And then I uttered the words I'd been so afraid to say for seven long, painful years. "For rape."

Pierce did not look surprised in the least when I walked into his office a couple of hours later. He held up a hand as soon as he saw me.

"I'm working on it, I promise," he said. "But there are a LOT of powerful figures at play here, so it's taking longer than it should."

"How is that fair?"

"It's not, Reagan. It never is." He shook his head. "But I'm working on it and will have him out as soon as possible."

I slumped down in the chair opposite his desk. "He won't let me see him." Pierce simply shot me an apologetic look and didn't say anything. "You've talked to him? Is he okay?"

He nodded, opened his mouth to say something, but changed his mind and closed it again.

"Just spit it out, Pierce. It's me." I waved my hand at the newspaper on his desk. "I assume you've seen it?"

The corners of his mouth twitched. "It's a very flattering photo."

I narrowed my eyes at him.

"You're trying to think of what to throw at me, aren't you? Always so transparent, Reagan."

"It's Ree, now."

"Ree?" His eyebrows shot up as he tried out the name, nodding slightly. "It suits you."

"My point is, it's not like I can't handle whatever you have to say. Because, really, can it be any worse than that?" I pointed at The Times. "Or the fact that the man I love is in jail?"

He sighed and sat forward, resting his elbows on his desk. "Dare is okay, as far as I can tell. He's a bit…abrasive."

"Well, he's in jail and probably thinks our father is trying to keep him there…which is very likely true." I sagged against the back of my chair. "What am I going to do?"

"You've given your statement, right?"

"Yes, last night." I leaned my head on my hand, and told him I'd also filed a report about the rape.

He looked surprised and maybe even a little impressed. "So," he said, "it's been a big morning for you."

"To say the least." I tried to smile, but failed. "I could have done without all this." Then I realized what day it was. "Oh, shit. I've still got the art show with the kids at the shelter this afternoon." I glanced at the time on my phone. "I should already be there."

I shook my head, not knowing what to do. I couldn't let the kids down. They needed people who came through for them. But with Dare and everything—

"Go," Pierce said. "Go, get your mind off of this. I can see it's important to you." I opened my mouth to protest but he cut me off. "I'll keep working on Dare's case, okay? I promise, Reaga— *Ree*. I'll call you later when I know more."

"The MOMENT you know."

"Not even a nanosecond later. I swear."

twenty
Reagan

As I walked the streets of New York, it felt like everyone I passed gave me a second glance, the way you do when you recognize someone. I felt exposed, raw...hunted. Especially after I noticed a few people taking pictures with their cell phones. Whispered conversations bombarded my ears as I walked by, and though I couldn't make out what people were saying, I was sure they were all talking about me.

God, I needed to get out of my own head. My body was aching to walk if only to break the exhausting cycle of thoughts circling through my mind, but I couldn't stand the looks I was getting. So I grabbed a cab up to Harlem, desperate to get to the art show as soon as possible.

At the shelter, I braced myself for more of the same, but no one looked at me any differently. The kids, of course, wouldn't have any idea what was going on, but even the adults didn't seem to know, or maybe to them it wasn't that big of a deal. They'd all been through their own personal dramas, and had bigger worries to deal with.

In the end, we were all human. No matter how you dressed—secondhand clothes or designer wear—we all had issues.

The show went beautifully, and the pride I saw painted across the kids' smiling faces made my heart swell and my eyes overflow. I kept turning to look for Dare to tell him something, only to be hit with reality again. I'd had crazy hope that maybe Pierce could have gotten him released in time and he would have surprised me by coming.

I was just starting to clean up—after being hugged and squeezed repeatedly by my kids as they said goodbye—when my phone buzzed.

"Pierce?" I said, not even giving him a chance to respond. "Is Dare getting out tonight?"

"Have you seen the news, Ree?"

"What? No. Is Dare okay?"

"It's not Dare—he's fine. It's Jackson." Pierce paused and took a deep breath. "Apparently after seeing the article in the paper this morning, several women came forward with similar stories about Jack, and they filed reports."

A cold chill washed over me. Oh my god. He'd

done it to others too? If only I'd said something, if I'd pushed my parents—

"It's not your fault." Pierce broke into my thoughts. "So don't even go there. This is on Dad and Mother. You and I both know that."

"But—" I took a deep breath, trying to collect my ricocheting thoughts. "So what's going to—"

"Jackson committed suicide."

"Oh my god, Pierce."

I didn't know how to feel—my mind was blank. Slowly lowering myself to the floor, I felt hot tears streaming down my face and my body was rocked by sobs. A mess of emotions flowed through me, but mostly relief that it was over. Really, truly over. Jackson would never hurt anyone again.

"Ree? You still there?"

"Yeah, I'm just…" I couldn't finish that sentence because I didn't know how.

"I know. Why don't you come spend the night at my place tonight? Then I can take you to the precinct in the morning—they're dropping the charges. Dare's going to be released tomorrow."

That night at Pierce's, I couldn't sleep at all. Every time I closed my eyes, images of smiling kids from today's show filled my mind's eye.

Despite the hardships their families were going through, those children somehow managed to bring happiness to the face of every mother there.

As their giggles echoed in my mind, I was haunted by a conversation Dare and I had several nights before.

"What would you name her...or him?" I'd said, my hands drifting to my stomach, dreaming of our future baby.

He'd shaken his head. "I don't know. But no 'D' names. There are already enough of those."

"And definitely no political names." I shuddered. "Quinn just went totally overboard with little Harry Truman."

"Poor kid."

"Right?"

Dare laced his fingers through mine, our hands intertwined on my stomach. "We'll figure it out," he'd said. "We've got all the time in the world to make as many babies as we want."

Except it was never going to happen. Dare had lit up when we'd talked about having children—it was clearly one of his dreams. And if he stayed with me, he'd never realize it. I couldn't be the one to take away his future, but I also couldn't just let him go.

All I could think that night as I lay there waiting

for morning to dawn was: I wonder if Dare was still mine.

I was outside the police station the next morning well before nine. Pierce had said Dare was going to be released around ten, but I wanted to make sure I was there for him when he came out—that mine would be the first face he saw.

That he'd know I'd been waiting for him all along.

I just hoped he still wanted me.

He had to, right? After everything we'd been through, I had to believe that we were meant to be together. Dare was the reason my heart beat every second of every day. The reason I breathed. The whole reason I'd had the courage and strength to become the person I was today.

In all that had happened, starting with how we'd begun three years ago, I'd come to believe that I was made for Dare. I'd never known anyone like him—so loyal to those he loved, so fiercely protective and willing to put his life on the line, to always place his family first.

Family was so important to him.

Which scared the shit out of me now that he knew we wouldn't be able to have one.

I glanced at the large clock in the square across

the street. Ten-thirty, but still no Dare. What the hell was going on?

That was it. I couldn't wait any longer. It didn't really matter whether I waited for him out on the street or if I was inside.

I ran up the steps and spotted the officer I'd talked to the other day.

He nodded as I approached the desk. "Good morning, Miss McKinley. What can I do for you?"

"I'm waiting for Dare Wilde to be released. My brother said he was supposed to get out at about ten. Do you know what the hold up is?"

A frown wrinkled his forehead as his fingers clicked along the keyboard.

He shook his head. "Says here he was released a couple of hours ago. Eight-thirty, to be precise." He looked up at me, his eyes full of sympathy. "I'm sorry. Looks like he's already gone."

Already gone.

Oh, no. No. I couldn't stomach a repeat of what had happened three years ago. This couldn't be happening again.

But then why hadn't he called to tell me he was out? I hurried out onto the street, my arm already up, hailing a cab before I was fully through the door. Why wouldn't Dare have waited for me? He had to have known I was coming. Pierce was supposed to have told him.

And why the fuck hadn't he called me this morning when he got home to an empty apartment?

I pulled my cell phone out right now as a cab pulled over to pick me up. Shit. Dead. I'd forgotten to bring my charger to Pierce's and now I couldn't even make the damn call.

"FUCK."

"Excuse me, miss?" The cabbie turned and raised an eyebrow at me.

"Sorry." I pocketed my phone and gave him the address, then sat back and wished the city would go by faster.

As soon as the driver pulled over in front of our building, I shoved money into his hand, then sprinted for the door, fighting to get my key in the lock, hoping beyond hope that I was not about to enter a half-cleared out apartment.

Flashbacks of Dare's empty apartment in Brooklyn three years ago flickered in my mind as my shaking hands finally got the key in the lock and turned it.

"Please, please, please," I said, throwing the door open.

My heart stopped, then shattered.

Suitcases stood by the door. A laptop was open on the coffee table, the browser loaded to a travel agency website confirmation page.

Dare had booked a ticket to Paris.

twenty-one
Dare

"*NOOOOOO!*"

My head snapped up as I zipped closed the last bag. "Ree?"

Running out to the front door, I found Ree on her knees sobbing by our luggage. I dropped to the ground next to her and scooped her into my arms.

She clung to me like she would never let me go, and I relaxed into her, so relieved she was home, kissing her hair, holding onto her just as tightly. Truth be told, I'd panicked when I'd gotten home and she wasn't here. I'd ripped the place apart, sure that she'd left me. That she was envisioning a future of me in and out of jail—just like my dad.

That was NOT the life I wanted for either of us.

The feeling of her in my arms filled me. Ree was my home, my haven, the calm after the storm that had been my life.

But she was so upset right now, which fucking broke my heart because I didn't want anything making her sad anymore. She'd been through enough already. It was time for her happily ever after.

Our happily ever after.

I pulled back so I could look at her. "What's wrong?"

"Everything." She shook her head. "I went to pick you up this morning, but you were already gone. And they wouldn't let me see you yesterday."

The hurt in her eyes was killing me. By trying to spare her, I'd made things worse. "I didn't want you to see me there. In jail."

Her lips parted as she shook her head. "What?"

"I'd grown up going on weekly prison visits. My father spent more time in an orange jumpsuit than at the dinner table. That arrest for battery…it was too reminiscent of him," I said. "And I don't want to be him. Ever."

"You're not," she said. "You never have been."

"I'm sorry, Ree." I couldn't look at her as I said this. "I was a fucking idiot for attacking Jackson like that. I put everything we've worked for in jeopardy." I shook my head. "But when I saw him on you, his hands around your neck—" Just the memory of it was making my blood pressure rise again. "—I went crazy. And when I got home but you weren't here, I freaked out. I called your phone but it wasn't on, and then I called Pierce, who told me where you were." I hugged her again. "So I've been waiting for you and getting things ready."

She pointed at the bags I'd packed. "To leave me?"

"No," I said, and took hold of her face between my hands, forcing her to look at me. "Baby, I'm not leaving *you*." I pressed my lips to her forehead that was now crinkling in confusion. "WE'RE leaving."

"What?"

"We need to get out of this city, away from your parents. We need to start our life right." I took hold of one of her hands, and got up on one knee. "Ree, will you marry me in Paris?"

Her eyes started to water again, but this time a smile lifted the corners of her beautiful mouth. "You want to elope to Paris?"

"We leave today, and we'll get married on New Year's Day." Her face lit up and she reached for me. "A new year. A new start. A new life."

"You still want to marry me even though I can't

have children?"

I brushed a tear off her cheek, shaking my head. "Ree, you're enough for me—you've always been enough. I don't need anything in this world but you.

As her lips touched mine, my world filled with color again. Everything was finally back in focus.

These last two days had been torture without her. Right now, I wanted nothing more than to take her to bed to show her just *how much* I was not leaving her, and stay there for a week, but we had a flight to catch.

Everything would be good in Paris. I could feel it.

Her lips moved with mine as I tasted her, drinking her in, savoring the sweet little moans lilting up in her throat. I let go of her fingers, wrapped my hands around her waist and pulled her into me. Slipping my hands under her shirt, I traced the velvet soft skin of her abdomen, let my fingers drift to the little shiny bump in the middle of her phoenix—the one last gift from my father.

And though I hated that he'd hurt her, it really was a gift of sorts—physical proof of the extent of her love for me. This woman in my arms loved me more than anyone ever had in my entire life. That she'd been willing to give up her life to save mine…it still slayed me.

I was hers forever. And she was mine.

"So, I take it that's a *yes?*"

Her grin broke our kiss, and I lapped up her laugh. "Yes, oh my god, YES. It's perfect." She gazed at me in wonder, and I itched for pencil and paper to capture her expression. "You're perfect."

"I'm far from perfect, Ree, but I'm all yours. Forever."

"Is that a promise?"

I nodded. "A promise. A sacred vow. Hell, even maybe a bit of a dare."

one week later
Reagan

"You're not supposed to see me before the ceremony!" I scrunched my eyes shut, covered them with my hands, and quickly turned my back to Dare. "Get out of here. I'll meet you at the church in an hour. I'll be the one in that dress." Keeping one hand firmly over my eyes, I pointed to where my dress hung on the closet.

It was a soft, shimmery sheath so light blue at the shoulders it almost looked white. The blue deepened thread by thread, getting subtly darker down the length of it until it was the color of a midnight sky at the hem. We'd found it our first day back in Paris at one of my favorite vintage shops, and the moment I saw it, I knew. It was love at first sight. The One.

We'd been in Paris for a week, back in Dare's old apartment in the Latin Quarter, and despite all the little logistics of planning an impromptu wedding, it felt like the honeymoon had already started. We couldn't keep our hands off each other, couldn't get enough kisses, laughs, and love.

From the moment I'd met him, I'd never been able to get enough of Dare. No matter how many minutes, hours, or days we spent together, it left me wanting more. Infinitely more.

This was love. True. Deep. Everlasting.

I sensed him behind me before I felt his hands slide over the silk of my slip. "Why are you closing your eyes if *I'm* not supposed to see *you*?" He murmured in my ear, sending sensual shivers over my skin. His lips grazed my shoulder, and I melted into his arms.

"It's…bad…luck." The room was swirling in the most delicious way. "We've had enough already. Can't afford anymore."

"True," he said and I felt the earth tilt as he sucked my earlobe between his lips, nibbling gently. "But something that feels this good can't be bad, right?" I nodded, unable to speak for the sensations he was inspiring all over my body as he continued to kiss his way down. "This will counteract any possible bad luck."

His teeth skimmed my neck, and my body started humming. Thrills ran down my spine, spurring on the throb between my thighs.

"Oh, god. If you keep doing that, we're both going to be late to our own wedding."

"Fine by me." He turned me around to face him, his deep, dark gaze so full of love that tears stung my eyes. "I vote we just get to the consummating part right now."

How did I get so lucky? Dare was my dream come true, my soul's reflection.

I reached for him then, because I was not capable of resisting. And when our bodies collided in an epic explosion of fireworks for the last time in our single lives, I knew in my heart that this was simply a prelude of all that was to come.

God, I was so lucky.

I hurried toward the church half an hour later, after chasing Dare out of the bridal suite. He'd zipped my dress up—only after I threatened him with bodily harm if he didn't stop trailing his fingers up and down my spine instead of helping me get dressed. He'd laughed, slipped his hand under my dress and between my legs, his fingers skimming my panties and dipping inside me.

"Already wet for me again," he whispered against the back of my neck, and I shuddered in pleasure. "Once wasn't enough?" His hot lips pressed against my cool skin.

"Once is *never* enough with you." But I turned and raised an eyebrow at him. "Though it's going to have to be for now because your sister—"

There was a loud bang on the old wooden door.

"Dare! Get your ass out here or you'll spoil your own wedding!" Dalia yelled.

"—will be here any moment." I bit my lip and grinned up at him. "She's helping me with my hair."

He ignored Dalia's pounding, turned me around, and slowly zipped up my dress as I held my hair out of the way. Then he took my long locks and spread them over my back.

"Don't do anything with your hair," he said as his eyes locked on mine in the mirror. "I like it just like this. Just like you. So beautiful and carefree."

So now I stood in the entryway of the old countryside church, my hair hanging in waves down my back, a woven, flowered crown with long white ribbons hanging from it adorning the top of my head. Dalia had made it for me and I'd almost cried when she'd shown me.

I had never felt as loved in my whole life as I did today. Dare's family had always welcomed me with open arms, but the intensity of their love had increased a hundred-fold with me officially joining their family.

Ree Wilde. I was about to become Ree Wilde.

I'd been looking forward to this moment all week long—no, all my life long, I just hadn't known it until now. My entire body smiled. Every single cell was singing and dancing as I stood in the vestibule, waiting for the music to start, signaling my entrance.

"Ready, baby girl?" Archer held out his arm, and I slipped mine through his, nestling my hand in the crook of his elbow. He smiled down at me, and my heart leapt in my chest. "You look incredible."

An attendant opened the doors and I gasped at the sight in front of me. The small church was lined with candles from floor to ceiling, front to back. They burned within the ancient chandeliers, lit up the walls, adorned the pews. Warm flames flickered all around me, painting the stained glass windows, making the art on them come to life.

Thousands of silver paper stars hung from the ceiling, illuminating my way down the flower-speckled meadow of the aisle. Large canvases were positioned along the perimeter of the small space—a sparkling brook here, a forest there. A grinning Dare was standing next to the altar, right underneath a big, painted moon.

Oh, my god. My dream wedding. THIS was my dream wedding.

I looked at Dare in wonder. He'd done this. He'd given me all my dreams. My soul swelled with more love than I ever thought it could possibly hold.

As Archer and I began walking down the aisle, Dare's smile grew wider. Up ahead Dalia, Dax, Dash, and Celia stood to the right behind him. On the left was Pierce, as well as Sabine, who'd come back to Paris from Berlin just to stand with me.

Quinn hadn't been able to attend because she didn't want to travel with the baby being so young, and even if I'd have invited my parents, they couldn't have been here. My dad was too busy trying to dig himself out of the scandalous hole that had cost him the governor's seat before he'd even had a chance to be inaugurated.

But I honestly couldn't have cared less. All the people I loved most in the world were here today.

My heart filled at the sight of them, but ached for the one who should have been standing next to Dare. *Rex*. My eyes sought out Dare's and he nodded at me, then placed his hand over his heart, like he knew exactly what I was thinking. My vision started to blur, and I tried desperately to push the tears away.

"You know," Archer said, squeezing my arm as we walked slowly toward everyone. "This isn't exactly how I imagined this working out, walking down the aisle with you."

Laughter sputtered up from inside me, and I stopped, threw my arms around his neck and hugged him tight.

"You know I love you, right?" I said.

"And I you, baby girl. I'm very happy for you…Ree."

Then I let him go and ran the rest of the way to Dare. With a deep laugh, he held out his arms, and I flew right into them, fitting perfectly, exactly where I belonged.

"I couldn't wait a moment more," I said, and pressed my lips to his for one last before-we-were-married kiss.

The ceremony and dinner that followed were a blur of happy tears and laughter, and before I knew it the day was over, and we were right back where we'd started—tangled up in bed together. My beautiful dress lay in a waterblue heap on the floor, his clothes were strewn all over, and we were warm skin on warm skin, lips exploring very familiar territory, bodies moving in sync.

I looked over at our laced fingers atop the bed sheets, now graced with gold bands that had flames etched around them.

Dare had kept them a secret. When I'd asked about rings, suggesting we shop for them as soon as we got to Paris, he'd said he had it covered, and wouldn't say any more. And when he'd slipped it on my finger during the ceremony, I couldn't help but gasp.

They were beyond perfection.

"These are from Rex," Dare had said, his voice tight, his eyes watery. "He knew I was going to ask you to marry me, and designed them for us. So even though he isn't here...he's still *here*."

The flames licked my finger, and my hand shook as I picked up Dare's ring from Dash's open palm and slid it onto his finger, promising not only my infinite love, but also my life.

Even after everything we'd been through, this felt like our true beginning. There was nothing in our way, nothing stopping us from finally living the life we were meant to have. The life we both deserved.

Gazing at Dare, and his family behind him, I knew that this was where I was meant to be. And that my life would always be blessed no matter what we couldn't have.

Dare was enough. He always had been.

And I was ready for our happily ever after.

one year later
Dare

"This is the one," Ree said, squeezing my hand and sighing. "The PERFECT one. I can't believe our search is finally over."

I raised our interlocked fingers to my lips and kissed her soft skin. "I don't think a better fit exists anywhere in the world."

The old farmhouse was *us* in every way imaginable. It had the vintage feel Ree was so passionate about, enough bedrooms Dalia and Dax would never have to fight over sleeping arrangements when our family came over to visit, not to mention floor-to-ceiling windows that let in so much light our current apartment looked like a dungeon in comparison.

We would be out in the countryside where I could paint in peace, yet could still easily commute into Paris every week. Which was crucial, considering how well Galerie Wilde was doing. Ree had opened it only four months ago, but her eye for unique talent had helped put the little shop in the Latin Quarter quickly on the map. A few prestigious clients were already clamoring for more paintings, more shows, more everything.

Our life was filled with art and laughter, and I couldn't be happier.

"*Mon dieu!* Look at all the natural light within this room! *Magnifique!*" Our realtor, Nanette, had a flare for theatrics. I could barely keep up with all of her high-pitched exclamations. "The space is perfect for a nursery, *n'est-ce pas?*"

Ree stiffened against me, her grip on my hand tightening slightly.

"Or a studio." I bent my head to whisper into her ear. "Where I can paint you every single day for the rest of our lives."

After the wedding, we'd briefly discussed our options for starting a family, but had ultimately decided to leave all baby talk behind for now—everything still felt too fresh—and focus on us.

Turning to Nanette, I said, "Can you give us a moment, please? We'd like to do a final walk-through in private and discuss whether we'd like to make an offer."

"*Mais oui!* I will be out in ze car, getting

contracts ready just in case." She placed her hand on her chest and let out an excited "Ohh!" then quickly clicked her way out into the hall, taking to herself in French.

I stepped behind Ree and wrapped my arms around her waist, pulling her into me. My lips grazed her cheek as I nodded at the corner across the room. "I'm going to set up my easel and paints there." I moved us slightly to the right. "And you're going to pose here while I paint you in the nude."

"*Me* naked or *you* naked?" I could hear the smile on her lips.

"BOTH   naked.   Of   course."   Grinning mischievously, I added, "And the best part about this place? No neighbors for a mile in each direction. No one can hear you moan and scream when I—"

"Dare Wilde!" She spun around and clamped her hand across my mouth, laughing as she peered out the window in search of Nanette. Her eyes dimmed slightly. "But what if you change your mind? About...me being all you need?"

I shook my head. "I'm never going to change my mind about you, baby. Ever." Taking her fingers in mine, I rested her palm over my heart. "Two parts, one whole. Don't you ever doubt that."

"Alright. This will be your studio, then." She wrapped her arms around my neck and squeezed me tightly, her sweet honey scent filling my nostrils and warming my whole damn body. "But how in the world are we going to use the rest of this space?"

Leading her by the hand, I slowly walked us into the next room. "This can be your office on the days you're working from home." Wallpaper decorated with tiny forget-me-nots lined the walls of the room, the dark hardwood floor groaned slightly when we stepped over the threshold. "What do you think?"

Ree arched a wicked eyebrow. "I thought on the days I'm home I'd be naked on your studio floor."

"True. Let me reword that…this can be your office on days you're working from home and I'm out teaching." I was finishing my second semester at Paris Atelier d'Art and loving every moment of it. My most promising student was Vincent, this year's recipient of the Rex Vogel Artist Grant. "Better?"

"Much." She gave a satisfied nod. "Now let's see the kitchen and how well the stove can handle our weekly mac and cheese nights."

By the time we'd finished a tour of the downstairs and were heading to the top floor, my phone buzzed.

"Dash again?" Ree asked, glancing over at my screen.

"Yes, he wants to make sure we got the tickets he sent," I said. "And he wants to remind us that this is the band's biggest show to date." *No Man's Land* had a full house at Bercy in Paris tonight, and both Ree and I were looking forward to seeing Dash, Indie, Hawk, and Leo again. Synner, on the other hand, had better stay the hell out of my way.

Ree nudged my shoulder. "Do you think Dash's little bird will be there?"

I shrugged. "I'm starting to think the elusive Wren is just a myth."

"Don't say that!" She smacked my arm. "Maybe tonight's the night we finally get to meet her and find out their story."

"Maybe. Stranger things have happened at Dash's concerts, after all," I said. "Once upon a time, I met a pretty blonde girl who—"

"Wanted to jump your bones," Ree cut in with a laugh.

"And here I thought you were looking for a prince in shining armor."

"More like a commando prince with a shiny—"

"Ree Wilde!"

I chased her sweet laugher all the way into the master bedroom where she spun around with a dazzling grin on her face. The smile lit up her eyes, colored her cheeks, radiated from her face.

"Once upon a time, two broken people found healing in each other's arms and a home within their hearts," she said, completely serious now. "That's the real story, Dare. Our happily ever after."

Sliding my fingers under her chin, I lifted her mouth to mine. "One that will never have an ending. I promise you that." My other hand grazed her shoulder, sliding her jacket down her back. "Now let's christen our fucking castle."

another year and a half later
Reagan

"What time do they get in?" I hurried into the living room to help Dare finish up. We'd been trying to get ready for Dax and Dalia's arrival for days now, squeezing in ten minute cleaning intervals whenever we could in between everything else we had to do.

And here we were—basically out of time. The twins would be here any minute and the place was still a mess.

Dust sparkled in the warm yellow sunlight streaming through the open windows as we worked together to neaten the room. I'd bought groceries that morning, and had already gotten the guestrooms straightened out, so the only thing left was this room.

We'd been living in the old farmhouse for the

past year and a half, and despite it being a bit of fixer-upper, our love affair with the place still hadn't worn off. And how could it? We had everything we needed. The beautiful French countryside out our windows and my favorite city in the world just a train ride away...life was so fucking good.

Hell, *good* didn't even begin to cover it.

I'd never been so busy and so deliriously happy in my life.

My little gallery was growing, making a stamp on the art world, and I'd had to hire a couple of people to help out recently. Dare was painting like crazy, trying to keep up with demand for his work. Even now, his hands were speckled with paint—some of it fresh.

He showed his work through Galerie Wilde exclusively—which I'd told him was not the best business decision for his career, but even so, his paintings were being snapped up, his name growing in the industry. He still taught classes, but had taken a few months off for our latest project.

I crossed toward the kitchen to grab a towel to wipe off the tables, but Dare caught hold of me, spun me into his arms, and dazzled me with the most amazingly happy and exhausted smile. I laughed up at him, and he reached out to caress my face.

"Have I told you lately how much I love your smile? It's the most beautiful one in the world." And then he leaned down to kiss me, his bliss mingling with mine, a palpable thing in this house now.

A car door slammed outside, yet I couldn't do anything but continue to kiss the man of my dreams. Of my days and nights.

"God, Dare," Dax said as he and Dalia came up the front walk. "Do you ever let the girl breathe?"

Dalia laughed. "This is what you were doing the last time we saw you. Honeymoon hasn't worn off yet?"

"Honeymoon's just begun, Terrors. And this one ain't ever wearing off," Dare said. And kissed me again. Hard. My head was spinning and my cheeks felt warm when he let go a moment later, and went to hug his siblings.

Dalia crushed me in a bear hug, then stood back to examine me. "You look amazing, Ree."

My hair was pulled up in a quick, messy bun, and my skirt and shirt looked like I'd slept in them. I looked anything BUT amazing, but at the same time I'd never been happier in my life.

Dalia, however, looked truly incredible. She wore tiny orange shorts and an off-white tank top that showed off her sculpted arms and gorgeous legs. Her long dark hair was pulled back into a loose braid, and she had the look of a wild cat about her. And something was different—I wasn't sure what it was, maybe a new confidence or strength, but she seemed even more herself than ever.

"How's work? Auditions?" I turned to Dax. "And, oh my god, how was your graduation? I'm so sorry we couldn't make it, but…you know…"

Dax waved a hand at me. "Yeah, yeah. I know. You had an excellent excuse—two actually—and it was totally fine."

"Speaking of excuses…" Dalia said, her eyes lighting up. "Where *are* yours?" She started tiptoeing toward the hall, but Dare stopped her.

"You," he said, then pointed at the couch, "sit." He looked at Dax. "You, too." Then he disappeared down the hall, ignoring their grumbling and complaints.

"God, he's gotten even *more* bossy," Dax said.

"Yeah, I didn't think that was possible." Dalia perched on the edge of her seat, watching for Dare's return.

I heard him before they appeared…the sweetest little coo that made my heart swell and overflow.

Dalia and Dax's eyes widened when they saw him.

"Oh, wow!" Dalia held out her hands, and Dare gently lay our baby in her arms.

"This is Rex," he said, pressing a kiss against Rex's velvet soft forehead. Dare squatted in front of Dalia, not able to take his eyes off his son.

Our miracle.

"What about…" Dax said as he reached out a finger for Rex to grasp, but I was already moving toward the hallway.

Toward the other part of our miracle.

Two parts. One whole.

"I'll get Rex's little sister," I said. "Phoenix has been anxious to meet you both."

She was still sleeping when I scooped her up and nestled her into the crook of my neck, breathing in her sweet smell. She snuggled in closer, her little hands grasping my collarbone, fisting my shirt, her little sleepy noises melting my heart.

This feeling—this high—was one I never could have imagined. And one I hoped to never come down from.

I was high on life.

On love.

On Dare and the two new parts of our whole.

a note from the authors

Can you believe this is The End of Dare and Ree's epic saga? We can't! Thank you so much for reading. We hope you've enjoyed their ups and downs as much as we have! Thank you for taking these characters into your hearts and loving them, rooting for them, cheering them on to their Happily Ever After.

We really hope you've enjoyed this final book in the series. If you have a moment, please leave a review for this book (and the others, if you haven't yet). Good or bad, every review helps other readers decide whether they might like this series as well.

And if you enjoyed the series, please tell your friends about it! Spread the love of reading with those *you* love.

Warmly,
Victoria and Jen

Want to be emailed when Victoria and Jen release a new book?

Get on the Mailing List!

Enter your email address at either Victoria's site (victoriagreenauthor.blogspot.ca) or Jen's site (www.jmeyersbooks.com/the-list), and you'll be the first to hear when new books are available. Your address will never be shared and you'll only get emailed when a book has been released or is newly available.

acknowledgements

We've got big love for our editor, Stevan Knapp. This series is extra shiny because of his eagle-sharp eyes, and we can't thank him enough for always being so thorough and quick.

Many, many thanks to our early readers and reviewers for being so willing to post your reviews quickly and in many places. That's such a huge help to us! And to all the bloggers and readers who have loved this series from the start—we are so happy you have come along on this ride with us. We can't express to you how much your support and enthusiasm means.

Super special thanks to our cheerleaders and champions who've been with us from day one: Jena, TeriLyn, Jolene, Helen, Nicole, Beth, Lorraine, Monica, Ivona, Tricia, Gloria, Taryn, Josie, Traci, Carol, Jessika, Krystal, Diana, Kristyn, Jennifer, Zan, Catherine, Amanda, Meli, Miranda, and Justin. We love you guys!

And lastly, we thank *you* for reading our books. You're the reason we write.

More Books By Victoria Green & Jen Meyers

SILVER HEART
by Victoria Green

There comes a moment in everyone's life when they must decide which road leads to personal happiness. For Dylan Silver, this is that moment...

For the past twenty-two years, Dylan has been living in her parents' carefully crafted world, always putting her own dreams on hold to play the role of a dutiful daughter.

So when her best friend coaxes her into a winter getaway to a mountain cabin, she sees it as a chance to forget about the responsibilities waiting for her at home. At least for a little while.

But then her past catches up to her—in the form of sexy snowboarder, Sawyer Carter.

Six years ago, Dylan bid goodbye to the only boy she ever truly loved. Now he's standing right in front of her, bringing up bittersweet memories and igniting suppressed desires as he dares her to be the person she has always wanted to be.

Dylan and Sawyer's unexpected meeting is a second chance, but will a girl who doesn't believe in fate and taking risks be able to overcome her fears of losing control and finally embrace the life she desperately wants?

Only one thing is certain: after a week in Whistler, Dylan's world will never be the same.

ANYWHERE
by Jen Meyers

Skye Whitcomb is running from her troubles, and where better to run than Europe? Fresh out of college, she makes quick plans with her best friend Paige and hops on a plane.

Of course, nothing ever goes as planned—at least not for her. First, Paige has to bail, and Skye's left to travel alone. Then she meets sweet and sexy Asher Benedict in Paris, and sparks fly after a night together on the train to Rome. He's all kinds of perfect for her, but the timing couldn't be worse since she was running from the altar when she left—so the last thing she wants right now is a relationship.

But Skye's about to discover that no matter how far you run, love can find you anywhere.

AVAILABLE NOW

about the authors

Victoria Green has a soft spot for unspoken love and second chances. A travel junkie at heart, she believes in true love, good chocolate, great films, and swoon-worthy books. She lives in Canada with her high school sweetheart (who's graduated to fiancé) and their pack of slightly crazy, but lovable puppies.

She is also the author of *Silver Heart*. When she's not writing hot and steamy romances, she writes Young Adult adventures under a different name.

Visit her online at victoriagreenauthor.blogspot.ca.

Jen Meyers grew up in Vermont, spent three years in Germany when she was a kid, and now lives in central New York. When she's not reading or writing, she's chasing after her four kids, playing outside, relishing the few quiet moments she gets with her husband, and forgetting to make dinner.

She is the author of the highly-rated Intangible series, a young adult contemporary fantasy, and numerous contemporary romance novels.

Visit Jen online at www.jmeyersbooks.com.

Made in the USA
Columbia, SC
02 March 2022

57088572R00121